SABEENA

SABEENA

a novel

Narendra Taneja

Vitasta

Published by
Renu Kaul Verma
Vitasta Publishing Pvt Ltd
4348/4C, Ansari Road, Daryaganj
New Delhi - 110002
info@vitastapublishing.com

ISBN:978-81-991712-4-4

First Edition 2025

MRP ₹ 495

This book is a work of fiction and any resemblance to any person living or dead is coincidental.

Layout & Cover Design by Shubhpreet Kaur
Printed by Vikas Computer and Printers, New Delhi

Contents

1

The cold, foggy morning looked mythical. The surroundings were distant, hazy, surreal. The winter murk was unusually heavy, transforming everything as far as the eye could see into unfamiliar shapes and forms. The landmark railway station appeared frozen—spectral and still. A railway watchman stirred sleepily under his coverlet, slouched on an uncomfortable wooden chair inside the security cabin. The milkman, peddling past the station through the mist, on a squeaking bicycle, was barely visible appearing like a mound enveloped in a faded, black quilt, wrapped tightly around him. Only the duty-bound ventured out. Stray dogs, cats and the occasional squirrel gingerly hunted for breakfast. No birds chirped or took to the skies in the overcast dawn. Trains had been delayed for hours, as the traffic signals—dim kerosene lamps—had become invisible in the fog.

But what caught Vikram's attention that morning

was not the mist, nor the anxiety of delayed trains that were off schedule, but a behemoth of a locomotive: a newly inducted six-thousand horsepower diesel beast, laying somnolent on the tracks. Vikram had never seen anything so imposing on the rails—not even in his wildest imagination. Even as he peered through the fog, the sun's pale and weak rays suddenly struck the horizon with immense force, piercing the mist and revealing the sky.

Rubbing his sleepy eyes, half in disbelief, he darted past everything—the flowering frangipani he had planted, the wired fences, the ditch for laying the water pipe—towards the jumble of rail tracks, his favourite daily ritual. He rushed to get as close as possible to the locomotive, only to stop a few feet from it, stunned. He whistled softly, bewildered at the sheer unexpectedness of this development. Until then, he had never seen anything except a steam locomotive on *'his'* rail tracks.

Such was his innocent passion for the railways, that he behaved as though they belonged to him.

Vikram knew of no other world beyond this one. The railways were his life—his universe. He loved steam locomotives of all makes and power: their traits and tantrums, their hunger to draw attention, their wings of steam-clouds and vapours, moving wheels screeching against tracks, then puffing out a violent shower of tiny particles of coal to scare away the uninterested. All done majestically, well-synchronised, as if conducted by some celebrated orchestra grandmaster.

Sheee...shooo...chchuck...chchuk...chchu chchuuuuu...

And gone—melting into the horizon, leaving behind a caravan of white and black clouds.

A typical steam locomotive, as it began pulling carriages to their destination, fashioning a play and music of its own, seducing all the senses with its elegant beauty. The whistle, in symphony with the gearing up of its massive middle wheels, creating a theatre of shock and awe, attracting wonder from the spectators all around, more stunningly so in the endless agricultural fields and villages being speedily left behind. At night, the show notched up to another level, as if the locomotive were a Sufi singer and the millions of twinkling stars in the sky its devout audience. Sometimes, the locomotive looked like a giant flying object that had descended from the sky to speed, stun and entertain the planet. For Vikram, life and love, emotion and logic, reality and illusion were all in the steam locomotive, and in the railways. All of ten years old, but a child, like very few others in the town, he had extraordinary, unconventional tastes, passions, and likes.

This first diesel locomotive had come as a gift from America—*Amreeka,* as the locals pronounced it—without any promotion or propaganda. Vikram hesitated, standing close to the engine for a few minutes before mustering the courage to move closer and touch the body and the intimidating giant wheels. He did so repeatedly, with intensity and concentration, as if he were a great expert carrying out a technical inspection.

Awed, he whispered, 'Good looking, thickset, modern. But soulless, no character, no personality—nothing even close to a steam locomotive—surely, this cannot be compared with the presence and strength of our steam locos.'

He climbed up the four-step white steel ladder of the loco to peep into the cockpit, and made a disapproving face, murmuring dismissively, 'It looks like a cage in comparison to the all-open driver cabins in steam locos. It looks suffocating and claustrophobic.'

He then shouted impatiently, 'Uncle, Balwant Uncle,' calling out to the middle-aged driver, who was his neighbour at the railway quarters, and a close family friend, 'Why have you brought this *Amreeki* engine here? Does it really have the power to pull all those gigantic carriages? It looks so fragile in front of our fleet of steam locos.'

Balwant, member of an elite group of drivers selected and specially trained to run the new beast, laughed contemptuously, '*Arey*, this engine is the *baap* of the steam locomotive,' and then prophesying, 'all steam locomotives will gradually be replaced by diesel locos like this American powerhouse. We are in the 1960s, the new age, the modern age. The future is here. All steam engines will soon be gone forever.'

Vikram Sarhadi felt his uncle's laughter resonating in his stomach. He clambered off the train in disbelief, crashing onto the ground by the tracks.

'So, this boring, box-like thing will replace the steam loco? How? You must be kidding!' he cried out, looking back at the driver.

'The Indian Railways means steam locomotive, coal and...*chchuk...chchuk...chchuk*. The steam locomotive will never die, never!'

The life and ambience all around was overwhelmingly railways—the wide world outside barely figured in anybody's mind. Almost everybody—from children to housewives to grandpas—knew everything about the railways.

Meanwhile, a crowd of two or three hundred people had gathered—all railway employees and their family members. They lived in bungalows and quarters owned by the railways, also known as the Railway Colonies. These were scattered on both sides of the tracks, with some colonies pressed against the main loco maintenance yard and the train shunting yards. For the people turning up in large numbers, seeing anything unusual around the tracks was normal. Their life revolved around the railways anyway. Most onlookers looked puzzled, while others appeared awe struck, and a few, proud of the new acquisition.

'I wonder if it will lead to the shutting down of our century-old steam locomotive maintenance yard, the pride of our railway township,' said seventy-year-old Mangal Singh, who had retired as a loco driver many years ago.

Although a small town, with hardly twenty-thousand inhabitants, mostly railway employees and their families, Tundla needed no introduction in large parts of northern India. Located on the Delhi-Calcutta trunk route, four train hours east of New Delhi, India's capital, it was a famous junction and railways township. Anybody who travelled by train frequently—and millions did everyday—had gone past its platforms, with their British-Scottish architecture, iconic AH Wheeler & Co bookshop and food kiosks. The station had a proud history, impressive colonial buildings with ceilings, distinct hanging fans, and was always busy, with an incessant flow of passenger and goods trains. Many locals visited the station to watch the trains, for an evening walk, or just for fun. Everyone was like extended family.

Tundla was home to over one hundred and twenty steam locomotives, which travelled great distances, pulling passenger or goods trains, and returned to their nest four or six days later to be serviced. Most locomotives had been given names and assigned to the best drivers to be looked after. Drivers took care of their designated engines affectionately, like they would their own child; they polished them routinely, and some even decorated them with garlands. A few of the locos looked like brides, overdressed and bejewelled. The drivers would paint or engrave their own name on the engine on a dedicated brass plate, located at the entrance to the driver's open cabin. It was common for drivers to invite their entire family to meet their machine.

Vikram loved *Chetak*, the loco that his father captained. He often assisted his father in polishing the engine's brass and copper control panels in the cabin. His favourite task was to polish—always with a fresh piece of cloth, carefully carried in his pocket—the driver's name plate, which spelled out his father's name: *Sudarshan Sarhadi*.

Vikram adored his father, parting his dense and black hair just like him and even dressing like him, in smart cotton trousers, a brown leather belt and a neat long-sleeves shirt, always tucked in. Like his father, he did not like short-sleeves, only folding his sleeves up to his elbow whenever it got uncomfortably hot.

Vikram had brown eyes and a sharp, slightly oversized nose, common to Pathans, a genetic inheritance from his father. From his mother, he had inherited her fair skin.

'You will be six feet like me—tall and handsome,'

his father often teased him.

'Our son is exactly like me—he's my carbon copy. Wait until he's an adult. He will look more like me than you,' his mother would contest, laughingly.

The two trains that Vikram rarely missed viewing daily were Dak Gadi, the Calcutta-Delhi Kalka Mail, with a red carriage carrying post, and even a letterbox, without any extra charge for faster delivery of letters and parcels to Delhi. The other train that fascinated Vikram most was the evening Delhi-Calcutta Deluxe Express, with the greatest number of air-conditioned coaches, with unusually large windows reflecting the soft lights inside.

'This train looks like a caravan of moons running on the ground,' Vikram often told his friends.

'My dear Sudarshan, I bet your son will be a driver like us one day, a very good driver. He loves everything about the railways,' Balwant, their neighbour, commented one morning. The two friends idled, soaking in the wintry sun on the lane outside the rows of their quarters.

Vikram's father smiled and said, 'I don't think so. I think he's made for better things in life. He's obsessed with the railways, but I suspect he will outgrow all this soon. Anyway, I don't want him to be a driver; we are all so poorly paid and poorly looked after, with no future prospects.' He sighed, thinking of how he was forced to accept working in the railways because of his financial needs. 'It was not easy to find a secure job for a refugee like me.'

Balwant suddenly looked pensive. 'You have a point. There's no future, or quality of life here. Our life in the railway quarters is like life in a Soviet commune that I have read about in newspapers, barely enough to survive, not enough to live properly and be happy. Not enough to even dream about anything or to realise your full potential.

'Maybe we should not let our children join the railways. There's a big world outside Tundla, a big, big world. Just look at life and opportunities that cities like Bombay and Delhi offer. We are trapped here. Our families know so little about the world outside.'

Sudarshan Sarhadi considered his friend's complete switch in opinion, and tried to comfort him. 'Balwant, it's not all that bad. The railways have given us job security and sustenance. But we should encourage our sons and daughters to look for better education, prospects, and jobs.'

Vikram's mother, Lakshmi, who was watching the duo quietly from the window of their house, sent Vikram with two cups of hot tea and some biscuits.

Balwant had a special place for Vikram in his heart. His only child, Sunny, would have been the same age as Vikram had they not lost him to typhoid in his infancy. His wife unable to bear the loss died almost soon after, leaving Balwant all alone.

Vikram, who had caught the tail end of their conversation, chirped, 'Balwant Uncle, have you seen Bombay or Delhi? I want to move to Delhi when I grow up. I have heard that it's full of bookshops, libraries and good colleges.'

'We should take him to see Delhi, Sudarshan. I will take you in my diesel engine, my son. Your father can follow us in his obsolete steam engine,' Balwant Uncle laughed loudly and hugged Vikram. 'I'm serious. Let us take him, Sudarshan.'

'Not a bad idea, I can try, but let me emphasise that I don't like your what-is-it-called diesel engine.'

'But, Baba, I gather you too have been selected for training in the *Amreeki* diesel engine! Is this true?'

His father, taken aback, responded, 'Nothing official about it yet, but I have been told to be ready for training at the school in Chandausi. Did your mother tell you about this?' he asked Vikram.

'No, no, a friend of mine. His father might be your boss.' Vikram turned to Balwant Uncle, 'but your diesel engine will not last long—it will soon be dethroned by the electric engine. I have read in the newspapers.'

Vikram's father hurriedly dispersed the meeting, collected the empty teacups, then placing his arm affectionately around his son's shoulders, he said, 'We have got to move with the changing times.'

The father and son duo walked back home to a sumptuous breakfast of piping hot potato-stuffed *paratha* that Lakshmi had prepared and served them with mango and lime pickle.

The primary school Vikram attended was a one-person enterprise—not a proper school as such, with no infrastructure, not even a proper blackboard or toilet. A thick black sheet of cloth nailed onto a banyan tree served as the blackboard and the shrubs behind as the toilet. The students carried their own little mat to sit on the floor, and brought their own bottles of water. A teacher, partially paralysed by a polio attack during his childhood, ran the school. Whenever the weather turned hostile, it had to be shut for the day. The school, however, was hugely popular and sought after as it was the starting point for most students who would then go on from here to crack the entrance test to the railways' school in the town. The teacher was good but tough; he had no tolerance for any indiscipline and routinely dished out corporal punishments like caning, slapping or forcing kids to squat with their arms through their legs.

Vikram hated the school, but cracked the entrance exam in the very first attempt and joined the reputed Northern Railways Inter College, Tundla. This was a secondary school for students from the sixth to the twelfth standard. The school had a huge campus with plenty of open spaces, hundreds of trees, good classrooms, and several fields for playing cricket and football. Vikram loved the campus, but hated some teachers because they did not appreciate his habit of asking questions.

The school had a geography room, which housed several world maps on its wall, and a few globes on tables. Vikram's favourite spot in the entire school was this room, where he dropped in several times a day to play with the globes and identify countries, oceans and mountains. His mastery over the globe soon became a game among his friends. His friends would cover his eyes with a large handkerchief, turn the globe hard and fast and then challenge him to identify some small country once the ball had stopped revolving.

Many girls were in his class, but Vikram noticed the teachers had actively told them not to interact with the boys. The girls were expected to leave the classroom as soon as the lunch break was announced. They assembled in a small hall opposite the classrooms, with many large windows, from where they would stare at the boys outside, giggling and sometimes teasing them, while waiting for the classes to resume. Vikram often wondered about this regressive segregation.

One weekend, he penned a short essay on the subject, entitled, *The Girls in the Cage*, and left it in an envelope for the school principal. The principal treated it as an offence and publicly reprimanded Vikram in the morning assembly the very next day. He was reprimanded for questioning the school's rules and practices.

Vikram was shocked, but not ashamed or disheartened. 'I did what I thought was right,' he told his father when the news reached him, adding that the girls' room did indeed look like a cage, and he couldn't help noticing. His father did not say much except, 'Focus on your education.'

Vikram assured him, 'This is precisely what I'm doing.'

Senior Sarhadi realised that his son was different from his sister, and even the other kids in the lane and beyond. Lakshmi also realised that her son could handle responsibility way beyond his age. She often sent Vikram to buy household items or to even bring a doctor if needed by the family or neighbours. Sometimes though, this maturity pushed his physical limits. Once, Vikram fainted while in a half-a-mile long queue in the middle of a hot summer day, waiting to collect ten kilograms of imported wheat from a government ration shop, during a famine-like situation across India due to the failure of the monsoon for three successive years. He had to be admitted in the hospital for dehydration and heat stroke—he survived— and the shocked parents decided to stop treating him like an adult.

It was a rule that was soon forgotten. Vikram was unlike most of his friends in the school or in the neighbourhood. He played with them, but his mind was always somewhere else, constantly curious, wandering and wondering about life in other countries and continents and even on other planets and galaxies. He was also obsessed with why some practices were the way they were, especially the discrimination experienced by the woman who came by every morning to collect excreta from all the houses, the girls in the cage, or why there were so many community and caste ghettos and stark poverty in pockets, in such a small town. He was a happy child, but he was also serious, intense and sensitive for his age. His parents sometimes wondered if he suffered from some medical condition or he was just a gifted child. Worry often kept them up at night.

2

Tundla was built almost from scratch in the 1860s by a British-owned railway construction company associated with the East India Company, a brutally ambitious, deeply exploitative London-based corporate entity. The Company had managed to forcefully capture and colonise much of India before the first Indian War of Independence in 1857, which triggered the developments leading to Great Britain proclaiming its sovereignty over the entire ancient land of India, or Hindustan, as the land, home to multiple sovereign or semi-sovereign kingdoms, was once known.

Tundla soon emerged as a landmark junction on the trunk Calcutta and Delhi rail route, connecting the new capital of British India in Bengal with major cities of north and north-west India. Over the next several decades, the British built Tundla into a small English-Scottish town with wide avenues, office complexes, sports and entertainment spaces and hundreds of massive bungalows, surrounded by acres of imported eucalyptus, native mango and neem trees.

Another unmissable feature was the mandatary rows of outhouses, shabby, poorly constructed, no-window, no-toilet servant quarters, attached to each bungalow. Typically, there were ten servants to each bungalow, catering to a *saheb's* daily needs. The British employees lived like maharajas.

Although it had been over two decades since the British left following India's Independence in 1947, juicy stories of *kale naukars*—cooks, cleaners, gardeners and horsemen—who lived in these outhouses and enjoyed illegitimate intimate lives with the white *memsahebs*, were still part of popular local folklore.

Azam Chacha, a hawker who sold kerosene and chicken eggs, a strange business combination even in Tundla, was a master story narrator and was the richest reservoir of knowledge about what British ladies did to stave off their boredom and loneliness. Their husbands were often away, either operating the railways in far-off outstations, or off on their fashionable hunting sojourns. Some of the women, Azam claimed, were particularly known for teaching western music and arts and making love to their servants.

'They loved Indian men like me,' Chacha would chuckle, his old eyes lighting up like an electric bulb every time he narrated a scandalous story, sometimes with graphic details.

Madam Murphy was his favourite in bed. 'My life has been a desert since the Madam left.'

The *Naach Ghar*, as the Friends Club was popularly known, was the heart of the town, surrounded by a beautiful church, a wide mall road, a basketball court, rows of bungalows and majestic trees on both sides of the central avenue, with the railway station on the one end and the ancient Grand Trunk Road on the other.

The club was where the Brits would gather every evening to make merry, drink, play games and dine and dance to a live band. The natives were not allowed to venture near the club on the mall. Scotch flowed like water every evening, elderly eye-witnesses claimed, with a mix of nostalgia, anger and regret.

'They would arrive by late afternoon and not leave before midnight. I suspect they had chosen to come here from their distant homeland only to have fun, make fast money and exploit us,' Raju Chauhan, who had served in the billiard room of the club for two decades, would often reminiscence.

The wooden dance floor was unused since they left, except for the occasional '*cultural show*' by the local children. The billiards room had fallen into the hands of local ruffians, who used it for gambling and boozing. The *Naach Ghar* stood disused, wasted, just like, The Institute, not far from it to the east.

'They built Tundla for their way of life—work, dance, drink, and fun. Our tastes are different; our culture is different.'

His contemporaries teased him, calling him a crank, a fake Englishman, a lackey, a traitor, someone they were ashamed of. Raju never reacted to these taunts.

The town had turned into a melting pot since those days, with many unique features for a town of its size and significance. It boasted of colonial-era clubs, a cultural hub called, The Institute, two lawn tennis courts, several badminton courts, two cricket and football grounds, a well-equipped hospital, many parks, and a multi-cultural and multi-lingual populace. Most of the residents were railways employees and their dependents.

Most families had five or more children and some, like the handsome Charan Lall, had twelve! The boys, who roamed around in juvenile gangs in their free time often ridiculed him—Lall was nicknamed the Father of the Calendar Army—the eldest son was called January and the youngest son December. Lall was illiterate—he could not even write his name. People like him were nicknamed *angutha chaap*, as they used their thumbprint as their signature.

Most drivers and their assistants in the cabin were illiterate, though there were several exceptions, like Vikram's father and Balwant. They were college dropouts, forced to take up railway jobs because they were refugees and had to accept any job that came their way. Most people in executive or managing jobs were well-educated, while many were overqualified for their jobs.

Eight houses were split into two rows facing each other in the lane where Vikram lived with his father, mother and a sister. Almost all the women in the lane were housewives, raising children, looking after in-laws, cooking meals, cleaning, stitching clothes, and weaving sweaters. Each house had two tiny rooms and a small veranda with an open courtyard in the back. The toilet was merely a hole in a crude raised brick-and-cement platform, with no water—neither stored nor running. People carried their own water in a *lota*.

Late in the morning, a young woman belonging to a very low Hindu caste would use her hands to collect and clean up the human refuse—visiting house after house, every day—her face covered—carrying a basket full of shit. Some families would offer her bread and vegetables from the previous night's leftovers.

Vikram often pondered about who she was and why she was kept at a distance. Often, he would chat with her hesitantly, picking a moment when they were not watched, warmly asking her details about her family, and at times giving her snacks. She fondly called him Chota Raja—little prince.

The entire area behind the railway station was known as the 'Loco', housing a huge steam locomotive maintenance yard and hundreds of living quarters for the workers and their families, employed to service steam engines in various operational and maintenance capacities.

The Loco was always full of choking smoke, soaked in the unbearable smell of coal and steam, from the engines being readied for their journeys. Its residents often fell victim to asthma and heart problems. Tuberculosis, mostly undiagnosed and untreated, was the biggest killer among the loco employees.

The Company Garden had a huge ground in the middle, divided into the beautiful football field and the *Ramlila Maidan*, which was the ground dedicated to Dussehra celebrations, the theatrical rendering of the *Ramayana*, the Hindu epic that tells the life story of Lord Rama, a noble and idealist king and a great warrior, who ruled parts of what is now India, several thousand years ago. Lord Rama was considered the ideal man—*maryada purushottam*, the most benevolent ruler and the ultimate god to many Hindus.

The football ground was the town's main sports arena. The annual football tournament immediately after the monsoon was a craze, so were the two competing cricket tournaments in winter—before and after Christmas.

Vikram's father, the head of the railway's local scouts

and guides unit, maintained and managed a small hut—the Scouts Hut, which served as the pavilion.

The two adjoining grounds looked breathtakingly beautiful during the short season of fog and mist every winter, with the Scouts Hut's gabled roof peeping over like an iceberg. Vikram loved walking through these grounds on icy winter mornings to think, refresh and rejuvenate.

The Company Garden also had two concrete tennis courts from the British era, tucked in a corner between the Ramlila and football grounds. They lay abandoned, as most people did not know what the two courts were meant for, and young kids would often turn up in the evening with their mothers to ride their tricycles. Even teenagers would join them on their bicycles. So, the tennis courts became riding grounds for the bicycles and tricycles.

The Company Garden generally housed bungalows, but Vikram's father was not lucky enough to get one; he was allotted a quarter in one of the recently built rows of identical houses, in a neighbourhood called the Quarters.

Highly religious, Sudarshan Sarhadi had mobilised other residents, and discussed the need to collectively rebuild a makeshift Hanuman temple into a concrete one at an empty parcel of land between their row of the Quarters and the Valmiki Basti—a ghetto of impoverished households, belonging to the Valmiki caste, who had been discriminated against for centuries.

A thick, high brick wall, nicknamed Our China Wall, stood guard between the Quarters and the Basti. Agile youngsters could easily jump over the Wall, but the Quarters' residents rarely did. The Basti dwellers, on the other hand, jumped over at will.

The Wall was an important divider, and Pundit Ji, who manned the newly reconstructed temple, was extremely sensitive to any intrusion from the Basti into his temple's compound, which he treated as sacrosanct.

3

The Hanuman temple soon emerged as the social and cultural hub for the Quarters, home to upper caste and economically secure railways employees. In stark contrast, the Basti—a kaleidoscope of discrimination, indescribable pain, and unpardonable social neglect—housed the men, women, and children of the Valmiki caste, or the Valmiki Dalits, the lowest of the lowest in the Hindu caste pyramid. Most fellow upper caste Hindus discriminated against them and called and treated them as "untouchables", which was against the law and, therefore, punishable. The Wall divided the two worlds. The temple, situated close to the Wall, was a no-entry zone for the Basti dwellers.

The *Basti-wallahs* and the residents of the Quarters never intermingled, or even spoke, except when the upper castes had to hire their services, always at exploitative rates—to sweep floors, clean toilets, remove dead animals and other such jobs that they looked upon as bad, dirty and filthy.

The Quarters had very basic amenities. The houses were built in rows of four, with plenty of space between the rows for kids to play and for the families to cultivate flowers and vegetables. Its residents were mostly low paid employees, working as drivers, guards, train ticket examiners, assistant station masters, stock keepers, telegraphers and clerks.

They were paid just enough to live—but never enough to save or enjoy life or go on a vacation—always a hand-to-mouth existence. Some amenities like housing, electricity, water, and education were subsidised. The *Basti-wallahs,* however, looked upon them as well-off, privileged and even powerful.

Aarti was conducted in the temple twice a day, in the morning and evening—an elaborate ritual in which a buttermilk lamp was offered to the deities installed in the sanctum, while worshippers sang prayers and devotional songs. During the other hours of the day, the temple's compound would transform into an *agora* for the children to play, fight, study and debate. Even though it was a Hindu temple, religion was no bar and even Christian and Muslim children entered the compound—but caste was a strict criterion. The Valmiki Dalits though Hindu by religion, were barred. The Basti children often stared down the wall, with visible sadness in their eyes, wondering why they were not allowed to join the children from the quarters.

The Quarters had residents from all parts of India who spoke various languages, practised different cultures and subcultures, belonged to many religions, and expounded a variety of thoughts. Vikram's neighbours—Henry, Venus, and their son, Matthew—were a devout Christian family. The family that occupied the house just behind their row were Sunni Muslim, and the one at the end of the row, facing the temple, were Sikh.

The Muslim children would often enter the sanctum of the temple and sometimes even join their Hindu friends to pray—especially during the anxiety-inducing tenth and twelfth standard school examinations, when everyone prayed—and at every possible holy place in the town, seeking higher grades. The Hindu kids could be seen praying at the *Syed Baba Ki Mazar,* the grave of a Sufi mystic, sheltered by a tall neem tree in the Company Garden.

The success rate in those examinations was rarely more than seventy per cent. *Pundit Ji* always supervised, and sometimes even encouraged that carefree bonhomie among the children. During holidays, children often played the entire day till the evening *aarti,* returning home to their families only in time for dinner.

The temple compound was large enough for about thirty-five children to storm around or study, without disturbing religious events or congregations or consultations with the priest. What the children loved most in the compound was the *chabutra*, the raised concrete platform under the big Ashoka tree, located at the entrance. The parents treated the temple as the safe zone for their children to play in as it was barricaded. The supervision of the octogenarian *Pundit Ji* was an additional assurance for the parents—even though the old man had glaucoma and his vision was quite poor. The parents nevertheless perceived him as a reliable guard.

Originally from a remote, impoverished village near Kanpur, *Pundit Ji*—whose name was Radhey Swarup Trivedi—had only his handicapped son left in his family back home. His wife had committed suicide by jumping into the holy Ganges soon after giving birth to their only child. That incident broke young Radhey Swarup, who once worked as a contract labourer on agricultural land owned by rich landlords.

He turned to religion and moved to Agra to work as the caretaker of a temple on the bank of the river Yamuna.

A chance visit to the Quarters led him to accept the offer to shift to his present job. He was not well-educated or particularly well-versed in Hindu holy scriptures or even rituals, but he had over the years cultivated a persona and mannerism that made him look like a learned and accomplished pundit. Always in his white *kurta-dhoti* and wooden slippers, he commanded respect and admiration among the quarters. Old-fashioned and orthodox, thanks to his background, he took all rituals and caste borders very seriously.

Pundit Ji was furious at Vikram one Tuesday evening—the holiest of all weekdays for the Hanuman devotees. Vikram had just gestured at Sabeena, who was looking down from the other side of the wall, to jump over and join the *aarti*, which was to begin soon. The priest always had a slightly blind eye fixed on the movements of the *Basti*. Vikram could feel the heat of his disapproval, but couldn't figure out why he was being glared at. The priest hurriedly wrapped up the *aarti* and let everyone assembled there leave, gesturing for Vikram to stay on.

'Why did you let that girl come inside the temple?' *Pundit Ji* thundered the moment the last devotee had exited, taking the boy by surprise.

Vikram had never seen this side of the old man he had always respected. The priest was shaking in anger. 'Do you not know the rule of the temple? No 'untouchable'...or what you call them now...V-Dalit... is allowed to enter the temple, let alone during the *aarti*?'

'She wanted to come in and join us for the *aarti*,' Vikram murmured innocently. 'Did I do anything wrong?'

Pundit Ji fumed, muttering under his breath that the boy was an idiot.

'Her name is Sabeena and she is also a Hanuman devotee,' Vikram continued, to *Pundit Ji's* agitation. 'She said she had always prayed from the back of the temple, from the Basti side. She wanted to see how the deity looked and pray in front of him. What did I do that was wrong, *Pundit Ji*?'

'Never ever do this again! Go home and immediately purify yourself because you might have touched her… touched an 'untouchable'…or whatever you call them now…Valmiki Dalit…calling them with a new name does not change anything. Old customs matter. No, no, no…hold on, hold on…wait here—I will give you a bath here, right now and purify you,' spluttered *Pundit Ji*.

Before Vikram could react, the priest hurriedly took hold of a bucket of water lying close by and emptied it on his head. 'Now you may go home—you have been cleaned and purified,' *Pundit Ji* declared in relief.

Vikram trembled with cold and confusion all the way home. *Pundit Ji's* rude, almost maniacal behaviour frightened him.

'Drenched! Why are you all wet? Did you fall into a ditch or drain?' Vikram's mother asked shocked, as she grabbed a large towel and helped her son dry himself. 'Did you fight with somebody who pushed you into the water?'

'I just tripped over a bucket full of water in the temple,' Vikram lied, trying to hide his own shock and nervousness.

Lakshmi was not convinced by so blatant a lie, but she could sense his edginess. Though she didn't say anything more, it left her worried and restless.

Vikram had a sleepless night. He kept tossing around in his bed, unable to figure out what wrong he had committed. He was aware of the divide with the Basti, but he did not understand how deep it was—how rooted, and how important it was for many upper caste residents in the quarters—especially for someone like *Pundit Ji,* an orthodox Brahmin.

The Sarhadi family's small, cramped house, had its entire household sleeping in one small room on bamboo cots, placed next to each other for want of space. Every morning, the cots were removed and placed vertically in a corner of the small veranda and the room rearranged for the day as a living room. There were only two rooms of equal size, with a small window, an old squeaking electric ceiling fan and a single 60-Watt electric lamp in each room. Power supply was always erratic—hurricane kerosene lanterns were prized and reliable possessions.

Lakshmi too could not sleep, troubled by the sense that something terrible had happened to her son. She woke up earlier than usual and decided to go to the temple to offer a special prayer for his well-being. As soon as she entered the temple, *Pundit Ji* ambushed her, demanding to know what was wrong with Vikram. Lakshmi, a regular at the temple, was not prepared for this avalanche. She stood there speechless and in tears.

'Have you not taught your son anything about our religion, our ancient traditions? This is highly irresponsible on your part—you are his mother! You are responsible for inculcating all religious traditions in children. Your son has no respect for our way of life, our age-old heritage!' he shouted.

'What happened, *Pundit Ji*?' she asked, haltingly, recovering her composure. 'Please calm down and tell me what happened,' she demanded, raising her voice authoritatively this time.

'You want to know what your son did last evening?' *Pundit Ji* roared, 'He invited a girl of an untouchable caste inside the sanctum—inside the temple's holy sanctum! An untouchable girl! Or…whatever you call them now…Valmiki Dalit…Breaking this temple's tradition, violating all norms and rules—this stupid, crazy boy,' *Pundit Ji* yelled, taking a deep breath.

'This boy must be mentally sick, under the influence of some evil spirit. He is not normal.'

Panting for a moment, he continued, 'But do not worry. I gave him a bath immediately. I'm also praying for him. He will be fine—he will not be punished by the gods for this sin, but we need to protect him from any divine curse. He should not have done this. He would not have done it, had you given him the right religious education. You have not been responsible enough as the parents.'

A number of visiting devotees looked more interested in the priest's outburst than in offering the prayers they had come for. A few barged into it, taking *Pundit Ji's* side. Emboldened by the support, the priest turned even more aggressive, his face reddening, his body language transforming into that of a warrior defending the long-held practices of his religion.

Vikram's mother stood there helpless and vulnerable, surrounded by the self-proclaimed *'protectors of the faith'*. In a town where everyone knew everyone, the priest had successfully drawn a line—all 'faith protectors' on his side—and 'the criminal's mother', as proclaimed by an onlooker.

Vikram's mother had never seen this side of her fellow devotees before. She felt as though she had lost her senses—there was a lightness in her head, a numbness in her body. A part of her was relieved, having feared something worse had happened to her son.

Recollecting herself, she cleared her throat and looked straight at *Pundit Ji,* and said solemnly, 'We left our ancestral homeland in a distant land—what is now Pakistan—for the sake of our religion, for our faith.

We know our religion well and probably better than many of you here.'

Everyone fell silent. Nobody had expected her to respond in this manner.

'We know our religion is big-hearted and open and all-embracing—like the infinite blue sky. We want our son to be a good human being, a kind person, a good citizen. That is what matters most to us, as a family—as Hindus, as Indians. Our religion teaches us to love others. It does not teach us to discriminate or hate. That is not the Hinduism we know. That is not what we are going to teach our children, because that is not what our gods teach us to practice. Hinduism teaches us *Vasudhaiva Kutumbakam—"The World is One Family".'*

Pulling herself together, she continued, now addressing the onlookers, 'We left our homes for our faith. We know what our children should practice and follow. Please read our scriptures. They teach us to love all and never discriminate against our fellow creatures.'

Pundit Ji was taken aback. He was not a true scholar—he had not read the Vedas or holy scriptures.

'Do not worry, Vikram will not be cursed, or punished, I am praying for him—he will be pardoned by the gods. He will be fine,' he babbled, now attempting to calm her down. He had not expected an intelligent rebuttal from a housewife. The visiting devotees never questioned him.

'You did not understand me, *Pundit Ji,*' Lakshmi said, raising her voice. 'You did not understand me at all.'

To keep the peace, she still bowed her head in reverence, leaving *Pundit Ji* with no option but to extend his right hand over her head in blessing.

Lakshmi decided to forget the entire episode and not to mention it to her husband.

***

Sabeena was the only daughter of Hari Ram, a floor sweeper, who worked for a private contractor in the railways. His job required him to clean the platforms at the railway station for over twelve hours a day with little to no break. He was paid a pittance. The railway contracting system was designed for contractors who were heartless and corrupt. These contractors hired uneducated, poor men and women from ghettos like the Basti offering no contractual protection. Without paperwork, the poorest were exploited and used like bonded labourers.

Sabeena had lost her mother to tuberculosis when she was two. Hari Ram was both mother and father to her, raising her with the help of his younger sister, who lived a few houses away in the Basti. She lived with her husband, eleven children, and her in-laws, in a tiny shanty made of bricks, torn rubber sheets and a tin roof salvaged from the garbage dump. There was no electricity, no running water, and no toilet in the house.

The Basti was densely populated—noisy, filthy and foul-smelling by day; rowdy and violent by night—loud drunkards and alcoholic husbands beating up women. In most homes, women worked while the men roamed or played cards under trees during the day, only to fight over alcohol in the evening.

A few days after the temple incident, Vikram spotted Sabeena at the *Achhut Kuan*—the untouchable well. She had come with a few other girls to fetch buckets of water. He thought of approaching her, but hesitated. Sabeena had noticed him but chose not to look in his direction as the other girls were around. Only the Wall divided the Quarters and the Basti physically, but in reality, the distance was far greater—like the Earth from the Sun.

Vikram might not have fully grasped the rigid caste order, but for Sabeena, who had experienced it first-hand, having suffered unimaginable discrimination, interacting with an upper caste boy from the Quarters in public carried serious risks.

The well used to be part of the temple's extended compound before the Quarters abandoned it having discovered that a few Basti families used it discreetly, in the pre-dawn hours, collecting water and, sometimes even bathing and washing their clothes. When word spread that the untouchables had used it, the Quarters, deemed it defiled and renamed it *Achhut Kuan*.

Gradually, the Basti women cut a hole in the Wall, for a convenient passage to carry buckets of water back home. Soon the Basti women had monopolised the well, making it an extension of their own settlement, much to the irritation and annoyance of the Quarters.

The Quarters shifted to another well, slightly away, known as the RPF Well, named after and maintained by the Railways Protection Force, which also had sweeter water. They had tap water connectivity, but supply was erratic and the quality of water, questionable. Vikram would still often fetch water from the *Achhut Kuan*.

He argued with neighbours who objected to his insistence on bringing 'untouchable water' home, saying, 'Nothing made by God can be impure or untouchable. The water comes from the same source to both the wells, why go to a well farther away?'

Sabeena was often at the Wall during the evening *aarti*, joined by friends, girls of her age. They sang the Hanuman Chalisa with as much devotion as those in the sanctum—eyes closed, heads bowed, bodies swaying with the chants. Sabeena looked more pious a devotee than most of the upper castes welcomed in the sanctum.

One evening, Sabeena stayed behind after the *aarti*. Vikram saw her, and gestured to her to enter the temple. Dusk had fallen. They hid behind the canopy above the idol of Goddess Durga waiting for all the devotees to leave. Soon *Pundit Ji* too departed for the day. Darkness blanketed the entire temple compound. Venus, always the first to rise in the evening sky, was followed by stars. A seasonal chill carried by the northern winds from the Himalayas drifted over the plains. The leaves of the giant *peepal* rustled. Sabeena and Vikram giggled nervously as they looked at each other.

Sabeena was a year older than Vikram—neither fully understood their minds, emotions or bodies completely—let alone the origins of prejudices or age-old traditions. Sabeena was dusky and tall, with long black hair and deer-like eyes. For a while, they sat in silence, lost. Sabeena looked happier than Vikram had ever seen her.

'You wear such wonderful clothes. You folks are rich, are you not?' Sabeena whispered, breaking the silence.

'Rich? Good joke! We are poor—maybe not as poor as people in the Basti. My father says we are lower middle-class,' Vikram explained.

'Poor or not—lower middle class or whatever—you people in the Quarters are different from us. You are superior, more fortunate, more privileged and empowered. My father says so,' Sabeena said.

'Superior! That's rubbish. Look at you—you are beautiful, intelligent, such pleasant company. So, who's superior—you or me?' Vikram countered. '*Pundit Ji* told me the same—that we are superior, made so by the gods. But I am not convinced. It sounds nonsensical and unintelligent. How can gods discriminate so criminally? Discrimination is a sin. Let's not drag gods into it,' he continued, leaving Sabeena overwhelmed, and in tears.

It was late, past dinner time. Sabeena and Vikram's curiosity for each other—discovering their minds, souls and lives—had driven them into a different world. They were hungry to know more—about each other and the world.

'You cannot understand how life is for a Valmiki Dalit. It is a life of daily insult, abuse, neglect and exploitation. We are denied basic respect that one is entitled to as a human being, irrespective of our social and economic status,' Sabeena said.

'Poverty, hopelessness, and darkness break you so deeply that you lose interest in life. It makes you feel unwanted. You age faster than others and die sooner. Thanks to the life and world around me, I feel much older and more mature than my age—I run the house like a grown woman, cook for my father, look after him, even protect him from nasty relatives who want to rob him of his tiny hut. I feel like an old lady, not a child. The locality I live in has robbed me of all innocence, of childhood.'

After a moment of silence she continued, 'I pray to my favourite deity, Hanuman. I pray for justice, I pray for help, I pray for liberation from this kind of life,

I pray for my father. But you people, you upper caste folks do not let the likes of me enter the temple so that we can pray, so that we can at least see the idol. I have to pray facing the back wall of the temple, like a thief. I cannot see the God I pray to, cannot touch him, garland him like you do. I am sure the gods hate upper caste folks for all that you do to us every day in their name.'

Vikram felt shocked and ashamed. He could feel her pain. Sabeena was not crying, but her eyes were moist. She was venting, in the security and comfort of a person she believed she could trust.

He wiped away a lone tear snaking down her cheek. He knew he could not fully comprehend her suffering, but he was disturbed and embarrassed that he lived just fifty metres away from the Basti and yet knew nothing about it, about those who lived there. He slowly got up and gestured for Sabeena to rise.

They felt as if they had just spent several seasons of life together. Vikram looked lost in deep thought. Sabeena, however, looked cheerful, glad to find a friend she could share her agony with.

Vikram walked her around the temple compound. He requested her to pray in front of the Hanuman idol for as long as she wanted. He also joined in, both reciting the *Hanuman Chalisa*. She stayed there with her eyes closed and hands folded in total submission even after the verses were all recited.

He then walked her around to other canopies housing Lord Krishna, Lord Shiva and Lord Ganesha. They prayed in the compound for over half an hour. The experience overwhelmed Sabeena.

Vikram helped Sabeena climb over the wall back to her home in the Basti. It was quiet, but Sabeena's father had not returned home, yet. Vikram's mother scolded him for being so late. He decided he would share the truth of the night with her, the next day.

He struggled to sleep, wondering, '*What is this world? Why is the world like this? Why are we, the so-called upper castes so insensitive and cruel?*'

Lakshmi had only been to primary school, but she was better than many college-educated adults in Tundla. The next morning, she cooked Vikram his favourite breakfast, *parantha* topped with a double omelette. Vikram was hungry as he had hardly eaten the night before. He asked for a glass of milk with Bournvita. Mother and the son had a hearty breakfast together, prompting Vikram to open up and share the truth of last night with her. Vikram's father would not be home until later in the day, driving home a prestigious fast speed train. His sister had left home early that morning.

Vikram started the story with his 'rather late discovery of the caste-based discrimination', 'the black hole called Basti' and concluded with, the 'very sharp, intelligent girl called Sabeena.'

Lakshmi's first reaction was a mix of shock, anger, and anxiety. 'What's wrong with you? Why must you land yourself into these situations? You are too young to get into such issues that even great reformers have failed to resolve. People don't think, they don't question, they just follow blindly, they behave like sheep.'

'Mother, why is Sabeena so dusky while I'm fair-skinned? 'Vikram asked.

'How would I know? This is all the creator's work and only *He* can answer such questions. But I have heard on the radio that it's all genetic,' replied Lakshmi, who was a radio addict, with interests in history, philosophy, and current affairs. A light green Panasonic transistor radio was her prized possession.

Vikram persisted, 'But how is everyone in the Basti dark-skinned?'

Rejecting the observation, she argued, 'There are a few in their community, too, who look as fair as you do. Even you are wheatish, not exactly fair. It is not about the colour of your skin, but about the structured social, cultural and economic discrimination against them, which has been going on for centuries, all in the name of religion, caste, tradition and purity. Any discrimination against our own fellow human beings is criminal, and importantly, in violation of the spirit of the Indian Constitution,' she emphasised, thanking her transistor for her knowledge.

'But ma, who are the Valmiki Dalits? Why are they treated differently, not allowed into the temple, or to share wells with us? Isn't it inhuman? Why does everybody seem to be okay with it, and accept it without questioning? How can such a practice be allowed to continue even after Independence?'

'So many questions, but let me try to answer. First, untouchability is illegal, banned and hence punishable, but we all know it's still there, everywhere, in most parts of the country,' Lakshmi told Vikram.

'In India, we have had the caste system for centuries, or probably millennia. I don't know. Originally, people were categorised broadly into four categories, depending on their profession. Priests and scholars were called *Brahmins;* warriors and soldiers were *Rajputs;* traders and shopkeepers were known as *Vaishyas;* and those responsible for cleaning, sweeping and skinning dead animals et cetera were called *Shudras.* Over centuries, thousands of sub-castes also came into existence.

As time passed, the original basis of the categorisation was forgotten and the category you were born into became your identity. Eventually, it evolved into a system including its discriminatory characteristics and features. What started as a categorisation got so institutionalised and rooted in psyche and practice as the caste system, that it has now become extremely difficult to dismantle it, despite many reform movements and very staunch laws against such practices.'

She sighed. 'You find this caste system even among Muslims and Christians in our society since we all share the same roots and practices. Hinduism is an open, liberal and all-encompassing *dharma*. There should be no room for discrimination or injustice in our religion. Untouchability is more of a social practice; we must all fight against it.'

'Mother, you could be a good teacher,' Vikram said, hugging Lakshmi, 'You might not have gone to school, but you are knowledgeable and enlightened.'

Now confident his mother would understand him; Vikram unabashedly shared every detail of his meeting with Sabeena.

The conversation helped Lakshmi calm her anxiety quite a bit, as she began to understand what was going on in her son's mind.

'What is our caste if we go by the categorisation based on the father's profession—and yours? Father, a railway locomotive driver, a steam engine driver? And, mother, a housewife?' Vikram asked her suddenly.

Lakshmi said, 'That is not how the caste system functions now. The caste categorisation based on what you did existed in its formative years. Now your caste is the caste of your father, not even of your mother.'

'So, *Pundit Ji* is a Brahmin because he was born to a Brahmin father, and not because he is good or learned?'

'Yes. *Pundit Ji* is poorly educated, not well-versed in the Vedas and other Hindu scriptures at all. He is slightly better off than me because he can read and write, and can perform the religious rituals, passed on to him by his father. He could not be a Brahmin, going by the original criteria of the categorisation.'

'I am beginning to get a hang of it now. Thank you, Mother, thank you!' Vikram hugged his mother in gratitude, before rushing out to play cricket with his friends.

***

The winter months were known as the cricket season, a legacy left behind by the British. India was among the top countries—all former British colonies—that had taken this sport to new heights and glory. Two different matches were going on in the cricket ground of the company garden. Vikram and his friends were playing in the junior's challenge.

Vikram was good at cricket, especially at batting, but that day his mind was not in the game.

'I feel like a big balloon has burst inside my brain, shattering everything, debris everywhere, raising questions in thousands—questions I couldn't have imagined yesterday,' Vikram said to Raza, who was fielding next to him on the ground. 'I am restless and want answers for all those questions.' His friend stared blank-faced and perplexed.

They lost the game.

***

Television in India existed only in a few pockets like Delhi and Bombay. Radio was common, but it was state controlled with content focussing on farming, social harmony, nation-building, current affairs and general knowledge, with three news bulletins in a day—morning, noon and evening. Tundla had no public library. The sole library at the railways' college was also poorly stocked. Vikram would eagerly await his family's daily copy of *The Hindustan Times*, published in New Delhi. It would arrive by the Kalka-Howrah Mail and was hand-delivered by early afternoon. The paper was fast emerging as Vikram's main source of news and knowledge—and more importantly, his window to the world outside. He would await the arrival of the newspaper like a hungry tiger. His father also had a small collection of books, but they were mostly in Urdu.

Vikram had a deep craving for information and knowledge. He often felt frustrated as he could not get hold of books he wanted to read and dig into—for answers to his ever-growing curiosities. He wanted to listen to—and wherever possible, participate in—

learned conversations on topics and subjects he was increasingly interested in, ranging from *what-is-life to what-is-death,* to philosophy, space exploration, international relations and the future of India. He often asked loaded questions on life or science to neighbours, uncles and aunts, attracted blank or irritated faces, at times getting rebuffed or reprimanded.

He once asked his neighbour, Mr Bankim Banerjee, why the United States Parliament was called the Congress, since the Congress in India was a political party. He did not know the answer, but to save face, fabricated, 'It is called the Congress in *Amreeka* because it was built by their Congress Party just like our Parliament was built by the Indian National Congress.'

Vikram listened sincerely and noted it down in a journal he kept. Later, he discovered that the information was factually incorrect. The Indian Parliament in New Delhi was built by the colonial rulers and there was no Congress Party in the United States. The episode frustrated him.

Vikram often felt like a thirsty camel hunting for water in a deep desert with almost no sign of it. He wanted to run away to a city where there would be libraries with hundreds and thousands of books and centres of knowledge and scholarship on various subjects. He was increasingly interested in real knowledge and scholarship, and not so much in a formal school or a technical career—fashionable in Tundla—like becoming a locomotive driver or an engineer. He would get bored when his friends would list their life ambition in terms of being just an employee somewhere, with job security as the only criteria.

'You guys are so predictable, so boring, so conventional,' he would often tell his friends.

***

Vikram spotted *Pundit Ji* walking back to the temple in the late afternoon after his ritual siesta at his hamlet.

'*Jai Ram Ji*, *Pundit Ji*,' Vikram greeted him in the colloquial fashion.

'*Jai Ram Ji*, my son. How are you doing?' responded *Pundit Ji*.

'Can I walk with you to the temple? I have some questions in mind.'

'Yes, of course.' *Pundit Ji* fancied himself a bit of a scholar of Hindu scriptures and traditions.

On reaching the temple, he offered Vikram a mat to sit on inside the Hanuman canopy, while slowly lowering himself onto a slightly cushioned mat, made of thick cotton, a gift from a devotee.

'Go ahead. What is your question?' *Pundit Ji* asked.

'Does our religion allow us to discriminate against our fellow humans, based on what they do for a living or their caste, or for that matter even their religion?'

Pundit Ji looked uncomfortable and somewhat annoyed. Collecting his poise, however, he began to answer, 'My son, it is not about what is permitted or what is not permitted, it is about what we were taught by our fathers and forefathers and religious gurus. It is about traditions, about what has been going on for ages. Who am I, who are you, to change it or question it? God willed these traditions and rules, and only He can change them—not me or any mortal.'

'But how could God have made such rules which discriminate between one human and another?' Vikram countered. 'These are not rules or even traditions, these are just bad practices which have not been questioned or removed. You are the head of this temple, you should take the lead, you can be the catalyst of this change.'

'I understand where you are coming from. You are still upset at me for reprimanding you for letting that untouchable girl…I mean that Valmiki Dalit girl… enter the temple sanctum. Do not be upset; what I did was my *dharma*, my religious duty. It is my job to preserve the religion, its traditions, its practices.

'Many temples in India have given up on preserving the traditions, but this temple is not one of them. I will rather quit and return to my own village or die than not perform what is supposed to be my *dharma*. You are an intelligent boy; may God always bless you. Our religion needs people like you at this juncture, people who know the art of articulation and logic, people who can keep their cool in all circumstances.'

Vikram told *Pundit Ji* he would like to borrow Hindu scriptures and epics to read them thoroughly. 'I believe Hinduism is a kind religion. There cannot be place for discrimination of any kind. It is unfair, against humanity, against the core spirit of Hinduism.'

Pundit Ji was smiling, as though he had heard all these arguments many times before. 'Ask the Quarters—will they accept your arguments? They will not, nobody will go against *dharma*, the ancient practices, the traditions. I like you since you can think, you can argue. But the door to the temple will never open for low caste untouchable people like your friend, Sabeena,' *Pundit Ji* declared firmly.

'I know her, but she's not a friend,' Vikram interjected, almost protesting.

Pundit Ji got up, abruptly, signalling his annoyance. He pulled Vikram's hands in his wrinkled hands, and announced, 'Places like this temple are meant only for upper caste Hindus—like *Brahmins, Rajputs* and *Vaishayas.* These people, who live just behind us here, in the Basti, they are all the lowest of the lowest castes. They do jobs like cleaning toilets and sewage. They lack hygiene and cleanliness. They are uncouth, drunkards, gamblers, and indulge in violence. Have you ever been there? Have your parents? Your neighbours? Anyone in your circle of friends? They are a different people—a different world. Hindus, yes, but very different from us.'

Vikram turned to leave.

'They all ought to be our own people—fellow humans, fellow Hindus, fellow Indians.'

'I like you. You are sharp, but stay away from trouble—and that girl.'

Vikram bowed down and touched *Pundit Ji's* feet, another ancient Hindu tradition, to express his thanks and respect.

4

No one Vikram approached in his neighbourhood had ever been to the Basti. It was, for all intents and purposes, a cordoned zone. All the Quarters knew was that every day, some women would emerge from within, walking with their heads down, their faces covered or half-covered, to clean dry toilets and collect night soil, which they would carry on their heads or under their arms to the outskirts of the town for disposal.

They also swept the lanes around the Quarters and sprinkled water to keep the dust from rising into the air. For the privileged residents of the Quarters, the Basti was not worth any attention. It was only during national or local elections that politicians of all castes and ideologies descended there—to bargain for votes with community leaders in return for cash, country liquor or cheap goodies.

Vikram had been restless ever since his first

meeting with Sabeena. Over the past few years, they had grown closer—meeting, discussing, debating and sometimes even holding hands in safe spaces around the Quarters. Vikram was deeply concerned about Sabeena and her future.

Sabeena liked Vikram for his openness, intelligence, and the fundamental qualitative change he had brought about in her thinking and self-confidence. She had changed so much since they first met, becoming more confident and profoundly positive. She also had strong feelings for him.

It was difficult to read Vikram; it seemed as if he did not have any feelings for her. But there was something—some pull, some attraction. This could not have been mere sympathy for her social neglect and suffering. Vikram and Sabeena looked as if they were made for each other. They looked so pleasant and complete whenever they appeared together.

Vikram asked his friends if anyone would like to join him on a trip to the Basti. None agreed, so he decided to go alone.

The Basti had about three hundred houses. Most of them were made of a mix of mud, old bricks and roofs patched together with plastic or asbestos sheets collected from garbage dumps. A few homes stood out, with concrete walls and bright coats of exterior paints.

All the drains were open and overflowing with filth,

human waste and offal. The lanes were so narrow that two people couldn't pass through at the same time. Buffaloes, goats, and pigs monopolised most of the Basti's open spaces, as they were important sources of income for most households. The *Bastiwallahs* treated the animals like their family, their own children. The ghetto had no electricity, no toilets, and no tap water.

Vikram was appalled. He had not expected it to be so claustrophobic, neglected and utterly unfit for human habitation. Not that he lived in a posh house himself, but the living conditions in the Basti were unimaginable.

It was late afternoon on a Sunday, so most *Bastiwallahs* were home or idling and gossiping under a huge banyan tree at the heart of the ghetto. Only a few tiny shops, sold daily provisions and *bidis*. Vikram felt uneasy, suffocated and unsafe.

'Who are you? Where are you from? What are you looking for?' A middle-aged man approached Vikram.

'I am from the Quarters, I'm looking for Hari Ram Ji,' the boy answered nervously.

'Hari Ram—the sweeper, oh! That old man, that cleaner?'

'Yes, the cleaner,' Vikram answered. 'I think he's a sweeper.'

'He should be around. I cannot see him here, but no worries—just go into that lane and look for the third shanty on the right, just over there.'

Sabeena was delighted to receive Vikram and introduce him to her father.

'Oh, you are that boy! Good to have you here,' said Hari Ram, gesturing for him to sit down on a low straw stool.

'I hope you are comfortable. You see, we are what we are, we cannot offer you water or anything—we know you are not allowed to visit us, let alone drink or eat at our place. I know. I'm old enough to accept that social systems are social systems—no point questioning them. I'm too old, tired and exhausted to talk about such issues.'

'Can I have a glass of water, please, Sabeena?' Vikram's mouth had run dry, his mind rife with nervousness. After drinking the first one, he asked for another.

Sabeena was thrilled to see Vikram drink their water, from their cheap aluminium tumbler. Encouraged, she served him some glucose biscuits.

Hari Ram looked at Sabeena with questioning eyes, as if asking, why is this boy here and is there something more to their relationship? He was old enough to know that any inter-community, inter-societal and inter-caste relationship could be problematic.

All Sabeena managed to say at that moment was, 'He's not like other people. He's a nice boy, different from the others in the Quarters.' The father didn't look convinced. But, as tradition goes, a guest is like God and must be welcomed and treated well.

Vikram felt overwhelmed—too many impressions, too many experiences to process, too many emotions to deal with.

'It is another planet,' he thought, locking Sabeena into an affectionate and sympathetic gaze.

'Sabeena is a very bright girl, gifted and intelligent. You must let her complete her education at a good school, and go to a good college,' he said suddenly, breaking away from the gestures and niceties. 'She's only a year older than me, but she's wiser, smarter, knowledgeable and very mature for her age.'

Father and daughter looked at each other intensely, their moist eyes sparkling as if celebrating the compliment coming from a boy of the Quarters, knowing such moments rarely occurred in their life.

'You talk like an adult,' said Hari Ram. 'My daughter is everything to me, she is my world. You must see how she looks after me. She is so much like her mother.' His eyes welled up with tears.

'Her mother left us too early; she died of tuberculosis. We could not save her. She was a wonderful human being. She was an anchor in my life.' He wiped his eyes with his arm.

'Sabeena does not remember much of her, but she looked exactly like her—the same nose, the same sparkling eyes, the same features, the same voice, the same compassion.'

After a moment, he continued, letting out things locked up in his heart for years. 'Son, we are poor people. No secrets exist in the life of the poor—unfortunate people like us; everything is in the open. Everybody knows everything about everybody in this Basti. People like us—we cannot afford luxuries like secrets. Those also are privileges reserved for the affluent.'

Picking up his thread of thoughts, Sabeena revealed, 'My mother, Asha, was Hindu, and married a lower caste Muslim, but she never converted to Islam. She remained a devout Hanuman worshiper all her life.'

'Sabeena's mother entered my life much later, after her husband's untimely death,' Hari Ram explained. 'He too had died of intestinal tuberculosis. He was a good fellow. He lived in a *basti* in a neighbouring town, not far from here. We were friends from childhood. He requested that I take care of Asha and their child Sabeena a few days before his death. He knew he would not survive. It is a very sad story.'

Sabeena rushed inside and returned with a black and white photo of her mother. All three looked at the picture silently, as if in prayer.

'My friend belonged to the *Bhisthi* community, and was very, very poor. I'm not sure, but I believe the *Bhisthis* are lower caste Muslims. Muslims also practice caste in our country,' Hari Ram explained.

'Many in their *basti* suffered from tuberculosis and other such diseases. My friend had no money to pay for proper medical treatment, otherwise, he would have been alive. Asha would not have contracted the disease from him and died.'

'Who are the *Bhisthis?'* Vikram asked curiously.

Hari Ram was not surprised. 'How would you know about a small poor community called the *Bhishtis*? They were traditional water carriers, supplying water to households in bags made of goat-skin, called *mashq*. They were mostly Muslim—I think they were all Muslims.'

Sabeena was named by Hari Ram. 'Asha and I never married formally, but we lived like husband and wife. That was what she wanted. She would say, 'What is the need for a formal marriage? It costs plenty of money.'

'For the Basti, for our community, we were husband and wife—we were a family, and that was all what mattered. Now, I live, breathe and exist for my daughter. My life revolves around her. I am happy if she's happy, I am sad if she's sad. My world is Sabeena.'

Hari Ram looked at his daughter fondly. 'I hope when she reaches a marriageable age— it should not be that long—I can find a good boy for her, a good *Bhishti* Muslim boy. I promised that to her father and I shall fulfil it. I will be ready to die once I have delivered on this promise,' he said, emotionally.

'What will be there for me to live for, once she

has gone her own way?'

'So, Sabeena will be married to a *Bhishti* Muslim only?' Vikram asked, looking at Sabeena with deep concern. She left the room, holding back tears.

'She does not know what Islam is. She has never been to a mosque. She just practises what I practise. But she's a wonderful girl. I shall fulfil the last wish of her father. I made this commitment to him on his deathbed.'

'She wants to study though—go to college,' Vikram said, hesitantly.

Hari Ram looked at Vikram queerly, as if silently saying that this was none of his business.

'It's time for you to rest, Baba,' Sabeena said, re-entering the room.

Hari Ram ignored her, and spoke to Vikram, 'Do you think I have money to send her to college for higher education? Look at my house, we live in tatters. I don't even have a proper chair in the house to offer you.'

Sabeena wiped her tears quietly, looking helpless, as if someone was reading out the story of her future and she had no control over it.

Poverty kills. Poverty kills your self-confidence. Poverty kills your self-esteem. Poverty kills your identity. Poverty kills your soul and body. Poverty kills your future. And 'untouchability' ensures all this happens to you.

Realising the conversation was becoming too emotional, Vikram stood up to leave. But just before that, he asked Hari Ram about Sabeena's devotion to the deity Hanuman.

The father's face lit up. 'That's because I'm a devotee of Hanuman Ji. So was Asha. I even fast on Tuesday as all his devotees do. I always pray for Sabeena's safety. Hanuman Ji is the only God we know.'

Father and daughter walked Vikram to the exit of their lane. People looked on, bemused, wondering what the matter was—that an upper caste boy had wandered into the Basti. Vikram could not help himself and asked Hari Ram, before bidding goodbye, 'What if she decided to marry a boy of her choice…?'

'Do you have a boy in mind who will marry her?' Hari Ram asked. Vikram fell silent. Sabeena too looked at him with a question in her eyes.

'Such freedom is unacceptable, unthinkable in our community. There have been several instances where families killed their own daughters trying to marry outside the community or against the parents' wishes. No, my daughter will never go against my will—and more importantly, against the last will of her late father and my friend. She will marry a boy I chose for her—a *Bhishti* Muslim. That was her father's last command,' Hari Ram said in a tone indicating finality.

Vikram thanked Sabeena and her father and took his leave. He walked around the Basti. Everyone seemed idle, staring at passersby listlessly. They seemed to have no real work, no occupation, no purpose.

The sun had begun its descent towards the horizon. Coal-fired stoves outside homes were being prepared for cooking dinner. Most households—even in the quarters—used coal, often hawked by organised gangs that stole from passing goods trains carrying coal, for cooking and heating rooms in winter.

Vikram went straight to the railway station from the Basti to watch steam locomotives and roam about and pick up the latest issue of '*The Illustrated Weekly of India*'—in an attempt to relax and destress. It had always worked—today, it did not.

He returned home exhausted, to his anxious family. 'It was very tiring, it was like experiencing a different world,' he quipped, changing clothes after a quick bath.

'But why did you go there? To see that girl's family?' asked Neha, his younger sister.

'I just wanted to see the Basti. I'm glad I went. The Basti is no longer a mystery to me.'

'But what was the point of the visit?' Neha questioned.

'I'm interested in the plight of the people there. How can our fellow humans live in such miserable conditions just because they belong to a certain caste?'

Neha was uninterested in the topic, and switched the conversation to another subject.

Their mother, Lakshmi, had been listening to the

conversation quietly. 'Vikram, you shouldn't think too hard about such issues. These things cannot be changed overnight. They were much worse in the past. Things are improving. Just think of this girl you talked about—isn't she an example of that?' She said gently.

The family sat down for a sumptuous Punjabi dinner, but Vikram's thoughts kept drifting back to Hari Ram, Sabeena and the people he had met or seen in the Basti. He wondered if they had eaten that evening—or even had money to buy dinner. Everyone in the Basti seemed to live hand-to-mouth, uncertain of their next meal. His own family though lower middle-class was still financially secure. But it wasn't class that bothered him most—it was caste. Vikram belonged to the highest Brahmin caste, placing him firmly at the top of the rigid social pyramid.

A few days later, Vikram approached *Pundit Ji* with the same question that had been weighing on his mind.

Pundit Ji smiled and answered in his signature *all-knowing* manner, 'God decides these things, depending on your *karma* in your past life.'

'How? How does He know the past, how does He decide?' Vikram asked.

'You must have accumulated good *karma* in your previous life—that's why you were born in a high caste Brahmin family. You have been rewarded for your good deeds in your past life,' *Pundit Ji* explained.

'We may be Brahmin but we are still only lower middle class,' Vikram persisted.

'Money is not what matters; your caste matters most. Be grateful to God that you are Brahmin. Money can be earned, but caste cannot. It can neither be bought or earned—you can only be born into it. That's in the hands of God. He decides which caste you will be born into,' *Pundit Ji* said.

'An untouchable person can make millions and he may still struggle for respect in the society. Higher caste brings you respect—education or no education, money or no money.'

'So, you are saying all those trapped in the Basti committed bad *karma* in their past life and that's why they are born into a lower caste?'

'Precisely. However, if they do go good *karma* in this life, they may get rewarded with birth in a higher caste in their next life.'

Then with a more serious tone, *Pundit Ji* issued a final warning: 'Stay away from that untouchable…that Valmiki Dalit…girl, Vikram—or be prepared to be born into her caste in your next life.'

5

The children were in a festive mood. Schools had closed for the annual summer holidays. May and June in Tundla were called the '*tandoori*' months, as mid-day temperatures would often cross 45 degrees Celsius, baking everyone, turning tree leaves brown and causing tar roads to bubble. It was common to see parched birds dropping dead from the sky.

For most, summer meant discomfort to the body, heart and soul. The appetite for food would drop to its lowest. Air conditioners were unheard of. Only the local hospital had a refrigerator. Possessing an electric fan was a luxury. The affluent few would escape to hill stations like Shimla or Mussoorie, but there were only four or five such families in the entire town.

The poor had developed their own techniques to beat the heat. A multi-layered turban on the head with an unpeeled onion underneath was a popular trick to protect oneself from a heat stroke. The streets were usually deserted from noon until early evening, during the hottest time of the day.

This continued until the first week of July, when dark monsoon clouds from the Arabian Sea arrived, carrying, cool air, then some light showers and finally, fierce rains. Monsoon brought smiles to every face. Rains were always warmly welcomed, often with dances, feasts and young hearts breaking into love songs.

Vijay, Madhu, Raza, and Ranga, had all assembled at Vikram's house on the evening of their first day of summer break. They were in a great mood, laughing, cracking jokes and sharing holiday plans. Lakshmi and Neha also joined in, serving the group cold Rooh Afza. The summer holiday meant either staying put in the Quarters or going to family villages to visit grandparents and extended families there.

Vijay was leaving the next morning for his ancestral village near Mathura, about three hours away by train. His family would be visiting their grandparents and granduncles and aunts there.

Vijay's family claimed to have ancestors living in that village for over two thousand years. His grandfather had told him they were Yadavs, belonging to Lord Krishna's clan.

Madhu's family village was near Kanpur. 'I am dying to go there as soon as possible. I do not like it here very much. The family village is where my heart lives. I have already made plans with my cousins to explore the village. I am good at climbing up mango trees and will go for the best and ripest of the fruit this year.' Madhu was grinning.

'The holy river Ganges is not far from our village. We will go there every evening to swim and chant *mantras* at the local temple. The Ganges water is always so cold, so sweet.'

Vikram sat quietly. Neha was playing the real host to her brother's friends. Neha asked Madhu if she could join her at her village for a few days next year.

Madhu, in a warm and spontaneous response, got up and hugged Neha. 'Of course! That will be so wonderful. I will introduce you to my family there—grandfather, cousins, cows and goats, our two dogs, our parrots! And we will go for a swim in the Ganges.'

Vikram looked contemplatively lost. He wondered, 'Why do they not call Tundla their home? This is where they live, study and play.'

He voiced this to Madhu: 'Why don't you call this place, the Quarters, your home?'

Madhu shrugged. 'The Quarters are rented from the railways. This is not "our home". Baba says we are just tenants here; we can be thrown out anytime. How can then this be our "home"? My father says that home is where your family's roots are, where your ancestors lived, worked and died. I may live here, but my heart lives in my family village; I love everything about my village. Home is always where your ancestors come from, where they lived, where they died and where they were cremated or buried.'

Vikram nodded. 'You have a point. Your father is right. I have read that even trees, animals and birds love and crave the land they identify as their own, their ancestors' home. All living creatures need a home, a place they can feel rooted in, a place they can recognise by the very fragrance of it. That is how nature has created us and wants us to live.'

Madhu, chuckling, turned to Neha, 'Your brother has started talking like an adult, like a mature man. All he needs now is a big moustache and that *admi-wala* look.'

Raza's family hailed from Zakirpur, a village an hour's bus ride from Aligarh, a town best known for its lock industry and the famous Aligarh Muslim University. He was proud that Zakirpur was named after his paternal ancestor.

'All our ancestors are buried there. You're right, a human is nothing without her or his roots,' said Raza, the only son of the railway's schoolteacher.

'A family that loses their connection with their ancestral home can never be at peace,' he said, sharing his father's words.

'I have no option—I have to go and stay in my

family village three or four times every year. Every time we go to our village, we have a tradition—we visit the graves of our ancestors and offer prayers and flowers. I love the ritual. It makes me realise how big and old is our family. I feel like a tree with very strong roots.'

Over the next few days, almost all of Vikram's friends had left for the villages they called their homes. It happened every summer, but for the first time Vikram felt a void. He missed not having an ancestral home that he could also go to. He wondered if Tundla was really his home.

'What happened? Why do you look so bored?' asked Neha.

'Nobody is around. The Quarters look haunted. I don't like it,' Vikram replied.

Neha was using the holidays to learn cooking and stitching from her mother. She was listening to Bollywood songs on the radio. She had also joined a class to learn to play the sitar.

'Instead of lounging around, you could pick up a hobby,' she chided her brother.

Taking her advice, Vikram decided to borrow as many books as possible from the school library on society, culture and politics. Students were generally not allowed to take away more than two books, but the librarian encouraged him to borrow as many as he wanted.

'There aren't too many who come to borrow books anyway,' she said.

Vikram began to venture into disciplines he was not familiar with. Sociology was new to him. Culture, politics and ancient history fascinated him. He began reading about the caste system, religion, history, philosophy and nature. He often felt the urge to discuss what he had read with someone, but Tundla was not the place for such conversations.

The idea, of what a home is had begun to occupy a lot of his emotional and mental space, leaving him restless and exhausted at times. He would go to the railways station several times a day—the place he loved the most. It was a sanctuary, where he found peace. The sight of his favourite locomotive or train was often enough to help him get his energy back. But the question of an ancestral home kept nagging him.

'Who are we? Why don't we have an ancestral home?' He asked his mother over breakfast one morning, with Neha looking at him, bemused.

'Ma, this is all coming from those heavy books he reads these days, and going around with that girl—I mean Sabeena. You should tell him to focus on his education and mingle with others and play like the kid he is. Even Madhu was saying Vikram has already become an adult, a full-fledged man, sorry an *old* man!'

Lakshmi shook her head at her squabbling children.

'Calm down. Okay, listen now, listen carefully, I must tell you this now that you are old enough to know: we are not originally from Tundla, we are not from this part of India. We are refugees from a distant land. We lost our ancestral home, our land, our fields, our money, our wealth and our livestock to the Partition, in 1947. We lost most of your family too—they were all killed because they were Hindus and refused to convert to Islam.'

As the children looked on, stunned, their mother sighed. 'Your father and I were very careful not to talk about our painful past in front of you. We did not want you to get biased against any person, any society or any religion. The Indian Railways gave your father this job. Tundla offered us refuge. We are grateful to this land, the people here. We are happy that we are alive, we are happy that we have you and Neha.' Her eyes were moist and her voice was choked.

Vikram was speechless.

Neha hugged her mother. 'Baba and you are our world, our home, our everything. Our home is where we four are.'

'Our future are you two. God has been kind. May you both focus on building a great, happy and prosperous future,' Lakshmi concluded.

Vikram's parents had been very careful not to expose their children to their life in what was now Pakistan, and the horrors and tragedies of Partition. Their marriage was an arranged one, performed with Hindu rituals in the Raja Bazar Hanuman Temple in Rawalpindi. He had been eighteen, she only sixteen.

They had hardly been married for four months when they had had to leave the land of their forefathers to save their lives—and faith. Sudarshan Sarhadi was at his ancestral home in Waziristan when Partition had happened. Lakshmi had been at her parents' house in Lahore. They had not been able to trace each other and assumed the other dead in the fire of Partition. They had reunited several years later at an ashram in Vrindavan.

As more details emerged, Vikram felt as if he had been hit by a thunderbolt. He needed fresh air and left for a walk in the Company Garden. Everything around suddenly looked strange to him. He felt shaken and uprooted. For a moment, he felt that the ground underneath him refused to carry his load, because he was not its own.

He was a stranger, a refugee. He felt the cuckoos and peacocks around did not recognise him anymore. He felt scared, abandoned. He was quivering from top to bottom and was drenched in sweat. He decided to go to the nearby Scouts Hut to drink water from a tap. It helped, but he soon collapsed there.

He had not been home for over two hours. Lakshmi sent Neha to look for him. First, she went to the temple, then knocked on the doors of a few neighbours. When she couldn't find Vikram, she rushed in panic to the Basti to bang on the door of an utterly surprised Sabeena.

When things seemed serious, Balwant also joined in the search efforts since Sudarshan wasn't home. Vikram was found at the Hut, half-unconscious, and running a high fever.

Dr Dinkar Ghosh was called to examine him. He comforted Lakshmi and Neha, 'Nothing to worry about. He's under some stress. Give him these tablets with hot milk. He will be fine soon.'

Lakshmi sat by his bedside. The scenes of her two dearest brothers being killed in Lahore kept floating in her mind's eye, haunting her memories.

Sabeena spent three hours there, helping Neha. For the first time, she had entered the home of an upper caste person. Neha served her sherbet and snacks in the family crockery, not in separate utensils that most families kept for lower caste visitors. Sabeena felt relief. She felt as if she was gliding on white clouds in the open sky as she walked back to the Basti.

6

Sudarshan Sarhadi learned of the entire episode on his return, after bringing the Calcutta-Delhi Howrah Express safely into its shed. He agreed with his wife that it was time for them to gradually expose the children to their family's tragic history. They were now old enough.

He himself had only now begun to accept the new realities in his calamitous life. He had been a pampered boy of a large, successful and prosperous family of traders and landowners, with a massive house—full of servants, camels, horses, cows, goats, dogs, cats and birds, in Waziristan—later named North Waziristan, bordering Afghanistan. The Sarhadis had lived there for several generations.

North Waziristan had a formidable landscape—eerie, jagged hills, and pencil-narrow passes and gorges. The region was known for its many tribes, which lived according to old caste codes and had long-standing family feuds, with vengeance passed down from generation to generation. Hindus in this region were a minority. The social architecture, however, was old-fashioned and worked in favour of the minority as long they were willing to pay the extortion money demanded by the armed gangs who styled themselves as local lords.

Sudarshan's great-grandfather was a large trader, exporting Indian silk, textiles and spices to Basra and other cities in the Middle East. He also imported perfumes, dry fruits and horses from there.

By the late 1930s, multiple national movements began to crack the social fabric of the region known as British India—which stretched from areas touching Iran in the west to South-East Asia, leaving it heavily polarised along religious lines.

The Sarhadi clan was confident that such a real division of the land along religious lines would never happen—citing the rich and long history of all religions and communities living together harmoniously. But many Hindu business families had moved parts of their wealth to perceivably safer Hindu majority areas like Delhi, Bombay, or Calcutta. The overconfident Sarhadis had not. Their prediction was disastrously wrong. They were targeted, killed and the few who survived had to flee with just the shirts on their backs.

In August 1947, British India was partitioned, with Muslim-dominated areas in the west and the east carved out as Pakistan. The rest became the democratic, secular Republic of India.

Over two million people were killed during Partition and over fifteen million suffered torturous displacement. Hindus fled to India for safety and Muslims crossed borders into Pakistan. This horrific history replayed in Sudarshan's mind as he looked at his son, who was still recovering from his shock.

Balwant dropped in to see Vikram a few days later. 'What happened young man? I hope you are off all medicines now.'

He turned to his friend, 'Sudarshan, your boy needs a change of *hawa-pani*. Let me take him on a joyride in my diesel engine to Delhi this Sunday. We will be back the next day. What do you think, my boy?'

Vikram thanked Balwant for the offer. 'I will sit in the cockpit of your diesel engine, in the jump seat, right?'

'Of course, where else!'

On Sunday, Balwant picked Vikram up from his house, promising a fun sojourn all the way. 'We're going in the same engine you made fun of! It will be pulling twenty coaches of the prestigious Gomti Express. We will be covering two hundred and five kilometres from Tundla to Delhi in four hours, with three scheduled stopovers.'

Vikram was excited. He was carrying a notebook and his father's Kodak box camera to record the journey.

The train arrived, and the driver exchanged places with Balwant, who formally took charge of the locomotive. He examined a few instruments and buttons on the cockpit panel. He signed and exchanged papers with the relieved driver. Balwant introduced Vikram to his assistant driver as, 'Sarhadi's son'. The assistant driver helped Vikram to settle down in the jump seat, explaining safety protocols.

The Gomti Express was soon dashing across the Yamuna-Ganges plains. Village after village zoomed past the window of the cockpit.

'This is so refreshing!' Vikram cried out, 'These villages look so peaceful, so beautiful.'

'I love these fields, green everywhere. The farmers grow wheat, corn, mustard and other crops in this area. I wish I could be a farmer. We were farmers back in North Waziristan,' Balwant reminisced in a voice full of pain.

'I wish Baba had told me and Neha about all of this before,' said Vikram.

'You were too young. Maybe he did not want to expose you to all the suffering he had gone through; maybe he did not want you to relive that pain. Now you are old enough to understand this world,' said Balwant Uncle, patting Vikram's shoulders.

On Vikram's urging, Balwant shared his family saga, explaining what it was to be a displaced family, to lose an ancestral home, their identity and the fields they had tilled for generations, to start a life all over again.

'It was a rebirth. Very few refugee families are in Tundla—a very small community. We all feel very lonely at times. Everyone is focused on giving our children a normal childhood and a healthy, happy environment. That's why we don't like to bring up and talk about our past in front of the children.'

To lighten the mood, the assistant driver, Shantanu Banerjee, took out a small jar of traditional Bengali sweets from his bag and offered it to both of them. Balwant Uncle too realised that it was all getting too serious and instructed Banerjee to prepare for the train's arrival at Aligarh.

Vikram got down from the engine at Aligarh station and bought himself a soft drink. He asked a coolie how far was Aligarh Muslim University. According to the books he had been reading, the university had been a central space in which the idea of a separate homeland for the Muslims of India had been developed. His impulse was to go and see the university.

'Vikram, hurry up. We are leaving in a minute,' called Balwant, dashing that impulse. Soon the train was running to Khurja, its next stop.

'Balwant Uncle, did the idea of Partition and Pakistan really germinate here at the university in Aligarh? Is it true?' Vikram asked.

'I am no scholar, but I have read that this university

was at the forefront of nurturing the idea of Pakistan. But I have also read that many at the university were against the idea of Pakistan and had actively opposed and agitated against any such move. I guess both sides of the argument flourished here. But Aligarh Muslim University now belongs to the government of India and it is rated as a very good university.'

'But Partition was such a painful decision. They partitioned such a beautiful country. It is sad that even Mahatma Gandhi could not stop them. I would have fought against Partition had I been alive then,' Vikram said, looking sad.

'Where do you get all this knowledge from?' Balwant laughed, trying to shake the boy out of his melancholy, 'From all those books you've been reading, am I right? Good boy. You should prepare for the civil service exam. You will make it—it is a tough, competitive examination to crack but I am sure if you prepare well, you will crack it.'

'I am not too sure if I will ever want to join government service. I want to travel, meet people, have conversations, see the world, go and study in the best university in the world. A government job can be too restrictive, however high a post you might secure. I think I would be unfit for a government kind of job.'

'You are beyond my comprehension, my boy. When I was young, we wished for a secure, well-paid job, preferably a government job because we thought a government job was safer than a private sector job,' Balwant told Vikram.

'But happiness in life is important—you must follow your heart. In any case, you have a few more years before you will be old enough to take such decisions. Enjoy my diesel engine in the meantime.'

Past Khurja and Ghaziabad, Vikram could see a forest of tall chimneys, buildings and electricity transmission towers in the horizon. 'We are approaching New Delhi,' announced Balwant, instructing the assistant driver to prepare for arrival. Soon the train pulled into New Delhi station.

The platform was at its noisiest, with passengers disembarking with their heavy suitcases, men and women holding on to their kids to navigate their way out safely, and redshirt coolies barging into coaches to help with massive bags.

Balwant and Vikram walked to the driver's overnight resting cabins, known as the Running Room. Balwant had arranged a separate cabin for Vikram.

After a short rest, Balwant took Vikram in an auto-rickshaw for a city tour. They saw the towering columns of Connaught Place, the iconic India Gate and the imposing buildings on Raisina Hill, which is home to the offices of the Prime Minister and his cabinet ministers, besides the palatial residence of the President.

Vikram also spotted the majestic Parliament House.

'Wow, Uncle, this is splendid!' Vikram thanked him profusely. Later, they had ice cream at the India Gate lawns before returning to the Running Room for the night, and back to Tundla, the next morning.

Vikram hugged his father tightly upon his return. He fed him the *Karachi halwa*, that he had bought from Old Delhi's Chandni Chowk. The sweet was his father's favourite. '*Karachi halwa* is a beloved sweet from the regions we left behind.'

More loaded questions were soon on their way to Sudarshan Sarhadi.

'Almost all our employees were Muslims; almost all our servants were Muslims. They were all wonderful people, they loved us, we loved them. Some have been working for us for generations. The Muslims who killed our family were not locals, many came from outside the region at the behest of their political masters,' said Sudarshan.

Lakshmi's family was from Lahore. Hers was a conservative family. She was not sent to school for formal education. Their house had been attacked by rioters at midnight during the early days of Partition, forcing the family to run for their life. She had been separated from her family, but another Hindu family had invited her to join them on a rescue train to Ambala.

Sudarshan pulled out an old map of the region to

explain the exact location of his ancestral village and the area. 'Let us first search for Lakki and then Bannu in the Frontier Province,' he said adjusting his reading glasses. Sudarshan took out a pencil and marked Bannu.

'Okay, let us now look for Miramshah in the North Waziristan area. Should be close by…found it, here it is, Miramshah.'

Vikram looked on, his heart clenching in a fit of joy and anxiety. He was happy that he would finally know, at least on a map, the location of his roots, the place his family originally belonged to.

'Our ancestral village, Ramkund, was about 20 miles south of Miramshah, not far from the border to Afghanistan. Let's see if we can find it shown here. No, it was too small a place. This is a rather old map too.' Sudarshan made a small circle at the place where he thought his village was located.

'What was Ramkund like?' Vikram asked.

'I would say Ramkund was both a village and a tiny town. Most residents were farmers and labourers, but there were over a dozen traders and businessmen too, with a long history of trading. Our family was in the trading business for centuries. Our house was known as the Sarhadi Haveli, built three hundred years ago and expanded several times over by the following generations. We had forty rooms!' Sudarshan's voice was both choked and proud.

'Ours was the largest house in that entire area, with servant quarters and guest rooms—and sturdy sheds for our animals. A corner on the roof was reserved for birds—where a little birdhouse was built. Our ancestral house was like paradise. I feel rootless without it. It feels terrible to be in the state I am in now—after what I was born into.'

It was as if a dam had burst—it was difficult, but at the same time, it was a relief to share the feelings that had been pent up over the years.

Lakshmi held her husband's hand. 'Your father and his family went through hell. It's a miracle that he survived—and is here, alive and sane,' she said to Vikram and Neha.

Vikram stood up to hug and comfort his parents.

Vikram brought a large sheet of paper and a few coloured pencils, requesting his father to try to draw his ancestral home and, if possible, a map of Ramkund.

'You know I am not good at drawing, but let me try to make a sketch of how our house looked.'

Sudarshan bent intensely over the paper. Thirty minutes later, he had sketched the family's ancestral home—three storeys—with living quarters on the first and second floors—guest rooms on the third floor. The *haveli* had three lamp rooms—one on each floor, where the help prepared dozens of kerosene and oil lamps at sunset—and placed them around the haveli.

'My father was very particular about the lighting of lamps in the evening. He hated darkness; he always wanted the house to be well-lit to look cheerful and happy.'

The *haveli* had a huge entrance with a wood-and-metal door. A smiling statue of Lord Ganesha sat on the top of the door on a small, decorated platform.

Vikram was both delighted and sad to finally see some version of their ancestral home. He lifted the sketch, carefully, folding it just as delicately for safekeeping.

'This is the most precious thing ever that you have shared with me Baba,' he said, tears filling his eyes.

Sudarshan was in a reminiscent mood; he told Vikram the story of a long, black snake in one of their water wells that nobody was allowed to harm as it was considered lucky for the family fortune.

'We would keep milk and food near the well before going to bed. The snake would emerge in the wee hours, eat, and go back into the well.' He laughed.

'My nanny used to tell me that there's no snake. All these stories were cooked up by the servants. She claimed they would eat up all the food that was put out!'

Then he leaned forward conspiratorially, 'On other occasions she would tell me that the snake is the ghost of a female snake whose partner was killed by accident years ago, when the *haveli* was being constructed. The snakes were madly in love with each other, and the female snake has stayed in the well, mourning her lover since then.'

Vikram shivered. His lips were silent, but his eyes begged his father to tell him more.

'Another ghost story relates to our overnight watchman, Badar Khan, who committed suicide just at the entrance gate. Many claimed that he still turned up every night with his gun on his shoulder, wearing his crisp white turban to guard the *haveli*. But I suspect those were just stories. It is easy for such stories to survive forever in places like Ramkund.'

'I wish I could somehow fly there right now, see the *haveli,* meet the snake and the guard's ghost. I will go there as soon as I'm old enough to travel. It's my life's priority now,' Vikram told his family.

'No, no, don't even think of it! Never even try to go there,' Sudarshan cut him off. 'It is history; it is all in the past. We now belong to this land, this soil, which has given us shelter, a job, food and life. You both must promise me that you will never try to go to Ramkund. It's not safe. It's a dangerous area. It was not that long ago that we were there. We were well known. Many people there hated us for being rich and prosperous,' he warned them.

'Are we Punjabi?' Vikram asked his mother.

'I am from Lahore, one of the biggest cities in Pakistani Punjab. So, yes, I'm Punjabi and you are a

Punjabi on my side. But I know the locals in Ramkund used to call the Sarhadis Pathans, or Hindu Pathans. Look at your big nose—this is called a Pathani nose,' Lakshmi laughed.

'Neha has a nose like mine. She has a Punjabi nose—sharp and beautiful.'

Sudarshan chipped in, 'Pathans used to be Hindus or Buddhists before Islam reached that area over a thousand years ago. Our ancestors refused to convert to Islam, but most did—almost ninety-five per cent of the local population converted over centuries. All of us—Muslims, Hindus and others—lived like a big family, like brothers and sisters.'

'But they killed your brother, sister, father, mother and others,' Vikram said sadly.

Sudarshan sighed deeply, feeling the ache of grief after all these years, 'A mob attacked my brother with swords, killing him on the spot, then my mother, and sister. They took away my father and killed him. Everyone was killed. Most Hindus in Ramkund were killed by this mob and the one that returned the next morning.'

Both Vikram and Neha wiped the teary eyes of their father and hugged him tightly. The family felt more emotionally closer than ever before.

7

The teenagers from the Quarters had divided themselves into two teams of eleven each. The cricket match started with Vikram at the crease as the opening batsman, with Madhu on the other side of the pitch as the second batsman. The cricket pitch—the field—was the lane that divided the central rows of the quarters. It was quite early in the morning, with the sun struggling to break out of the thinning fog and clouds, the perfect weather for cricket. Boys and girls waited now for an entire year for such winter days to bring out their cricket kits. The British might have invented cricket, but it was now the most beloved sport in India—graduating to the status of, well, almost a religion.

Vikram had scored eighty-nine runs and Madhu, seventy-six; both of them were in a hurry to hit a century each. Vikram tried to hit a six on an easy ball, but it accidentally hit Madhu's mother, on her right shoulder.

She was watching her daughter from the kitchen garden in the front of her quarter. She was not seriously hurt, but she exploded, screaming expletives at Vikram and marching threateningly towards him, pushing away the wickets and hitting the boy hard on his nose.

'How dare you hit me! I know you hit me deliberately. You uncouth, uncivilised refugee, no manners, no religion, no customs!'

Vikram was stunned. 'I am sorry. I apologise. I did not mean to hurt you.'

But Madhu's mother's tirade continued. This was not the first time she had been upset with him. She had singled out Vikram for such treatment several times in the past. She hated the Sarhadis because she thought they were too liberal and did not gel well with her idea of good social behaviour, sensitivities and religious traditions and customs.

She came from a deep and orthodox village and could not adapt to anything new. Madhu's mingling with the boys and playing outdoor games like cricket was already too much for her to digest. Madhu and Vikram were close pals.

'Such behaviour means you have no character; you are a loose character,' she reprimanded her daughter daily. She blamed the Sarhadis and Vikram for her losing all control over her otherwise wonderful daughter.

Her mother's attitude was not allowing Madhu to

tap into her real potential. She was caught between two bridges—the one she wanted to climb to build a brighter life in some big city—and the other that her parents wanted for her—marriage, children and being a housewife. Madhu was bubbly and ambitious, but the constant battles at home were destroying her.

Madhu tried to intervene gently, pushing her mother towards their home, but the lady would have none of it. She shouted at her daughter and then slapped her. 'You have fallen under the bad influence of this refugee. This boy is characterless. Who does not know about his love affair with that untouchable girl? This boy has no *sanskar*, no culture, no manners!'

'Mummy, stop this nonsense. Stop please,' Madhu pleaded. 'It's so embarrassing.'

'Stop talking to Vikram. No girl should talk with this rootless, mannerless boy,' the lady bellowed, addressing the passers-by that had gathered following the commotion.

Vikram's mother, who had rushed out from her kitchen, begged with the woman to stop and calm down. 'You have no idea about what you are saying. Come back to your senses, control your anger,' Lakshmi pleaded in her soft voice.

But the woman had lost control of herself. She kept targeting Vikram for his family's refugee background and his alleged relationship with Sabeena. Madhu was crying in shame and looked as if she wanted to find a place to hide.

Vikram decided he had had enough. 'Stop, Aunty, enough!' he screamed back. 'What is your problem, Aunty? Stop calling me a refugee, otherwise, I will also start calling you names. A cricket ball hit you. I said sorry. That should have been the end of it. What does my family's refugee background have to do with the ball accidentally hitting you?'

'It is because displaced people like you have a sick mind; you people get pleasure in hitting innocents like me. You hit me deliberately because you do not like people like me. You envy us for our rooted and grounded life. You want to corrupt our girls, our local culture, otherwise you wouldn't break all social rules and norms and befriend an untouchable girl, call her to your house and offer her a drink in your own utensils. Is this not a revolt against the age-old traditions, our local culture, our traditions here, in this town that has given you refuge?' Madhu's mother spat.

'You are the crudest person I could have ever even imagined. Please go home and rest. You have a problem with my refugee background, that's the issue. You have a problem with my liberal, modern thinking. The cricket ball was just an excuse,' Vikram said coldly.

He turned to Madhu. 'I feel sorry for you,' he said, softly. 'A sensitive and wonderful girl like you deserves a better mother.'

Such commotions were uncommon in the Quarters. Vikram and Madhu looked into each other's eyes sadly, apologetically. They agreed to resume the game the next weekend. Vikram later saw a doctor visiting Madhu's house as she had developed a fever.

Madhu recovered quickly and dropped in to spend some time with Vikram and Neha, disobeying her mother's stern order. She apologised profusely to Lakshmi, explaining, 'My mother is a bit crude unfortunately—not the kind I could be proud of, but a mother is a mother.'

Many in the Quarters belonged to Bengal, Kerala, Maharashtra and other parts of the country, and they were excellent in assimilating into one large family made of railway employees, often ignoring and overriding their other identities. They all worked for the railways; they were like one large community.

More than half of them, however, belonged to villages and regions around Tundla. They spoke local dialects, observed local traditions and festivals, and had some unique and delicious cuisines of their own. Sometimes, they behaved as if they were the only authentic residents of Tundla, the rightful guardians of local traditions, dialects, songs, and folklores. Others, being guests, were therefore expected to live within their limits.

Madhu's mother, a local, was again seen spitting

venom from her window, with no audience in sight. 'They were thrown away by the Muslims in Pakistan. They have now come here to corrupt our traditional ways of life, our girls. They want our girls to be like them—characterless and disobeying their parents!'

Lakshmi consoled Vikram, advising him to forgive and ignore her. 'Everybody is not like her. Look, even her own daughter is not like her.'

Vikram, who had become very sensitive since that incident, noticed that a few others in the Quarters looked at his family differently and sometimes posed strange questions.

'Why don't you speak in the local dialect at home? In which language do your parents speak to each other?' Raj Bahadur Tomar, who lived in the row of quarters behind the Sarhadis, asked Vikram one evening. 'Why did you people run away from Pakistan?'

'Uncle, kindly read some history. The home we had to leave behind was in united India, not in Pakistan, which was carved out after the 1947 Partition,' Vikram answered, irritated.

'Okay, okay, but how does it feel like to live like a gypsy—no roots, no village, no place to call home,' asked Tomar with a smirk, adding, 'I sympathise with homeless and unfortunate people like you, floating from one place to another just to survive.'

Vikram ignored his words. But these recent episodes

had left him upset and sad. 'What is wrong with these people?' he asked himself in despair. 'I was born in Tundla, these people have known me since I was born. Why this effort to *'other'* us?'

Over the next few years, Vikram would read more and more about the area called Waziristan, especially its history over the last seven hundred years and the rise of Islam. He continued to wish that India was never partitioned and the killings had never happened. He wished he had been born in his ancestral home and village—Ramkund. The assaults and questions of Madhu's mother and the ticket collector had left him disenchanted with the people around him.

Tundla was always home for Vikram, but incidents like these deepened his longing for having an ancestral home like his other friends. Tundla was his reality. Ramkund was just a fantasy now, given the situation of India and Pakistan relations. He recognised that, and yet his yearning for Ramkund refused to subside.

The weekend after the cricket incident, Vikram and Madhu returned to the crease, but Vikram was bowled out by Saya on the very first ball. Madhu went on to hit a century. Vijay, Suresh, Mahendra, Sunil, Yogendra, Nupur, Mohammed, Tara, and Harsh, also played very well. Sabeena was among the spectators cheering Vikram and Madhu's team, Both the teams had a great time, with no untoward incident this time. Vikram and

Madhu's team lost to Vijay and Saya's team. But both sides left the playground so happy and bubbly that it was difficult to distinguish who had won or lost.

The following Tuesday was *Amavasya*, the night of no moon in the sky. Vikram and Sabeena had agreed to meet for a long walk soon after the evening *aarti* at the temple. All the devotees had left. *Pundit Ji* left as well, putting out all the lamps. Sabeena finally turned up on the wall, looking hassled and tired, her eyes teary and red.

'What happened?' asked Vikram, concerned, taking her hand in his.

'Bapu is forcing me to get married to some boy from some family he knows well. He says he will not survive long from his illness. He wants to push me into some hell so that he can die peacefully,' said Sabeena.

'He wants to get rid of me—marry me off and believe that I will be happy and safe thereafter—so he can then die peacefully. All poor families want to marry off their daughters at the soonest—not to secure their future—but to secure their own peace! They may love their daughter, but a daughter is still a burden, a liability. It is so humiliating.'

After a moment of silence, she continued, 'Poverty is the biggest disease of all. Bapu has, I suspect, no option but to go with the stream, to be like the society he was born into. He does not have strength, mental or physical, to challenge it.'

The two headed towards New Colony, on the western side of the Company Garden. The town was enveloped in complete darkness. The streetlights, far and few, were mostly out of order. The darkness did not bother the residents much—they were used to it.

'For my father, a girl's sole purpose in life should be to get married as fast as possible, leave the parents' house forever and produce children and cook food for her husband,' Sabeena lamented. 'Everybody thinks like that in the Basti. I should not single him out. But what about what I think, what I dream, what I want out my life?'

'Why blame only your Basti? Most even in the Quarters think exactly like that. I bet most do. I suspect more than eighty per cent of Tundla thinks like that only. They look upon a girl child as a burden, a liability—the sooner you marry her off, the better it is. It is so disgusting. My sister, Neha, will do what she wants to do with her life. She will have full support from my parents and me.'

Sabeena clutched Vikram's arm. 'My father has started cursing me for my friendship with you, for the changes in my outlook, for my new-found confidence, for me reading more,' she shared. 'He says I will soon regret it all, because I will remain neither a Basti girl, nor belong to the Quarters.'

There was a moment of silence. Vikram decided to change the subject and began telling Sabeena about the cricket incident. 'Why do some people in the Quarters treat me differently, refusing to accept me as one of them, calling me a refugee? It hurts me deeply.'

'Others may not care about such things, but I do—I am very sensitive to such things. I was born here, here in this soil,' he said. 'My family lost their ancestral home, in the Partition. I often cry for that loss. I want my ancestral home back. I want to have that joy and enjoy the pleasures of having an ancestral village like Madhu, Raza and the others.

'I love Ramkund, which I know we will never be able to return to, but the way some people treat me, it breaks my heart and soul. I was born here, I belong to this *mitti*, this soil. I am still a young boy, inexperienced in matters of life, raw in emotions. It is only natural that I long for the land my family originally came from, that I still relate to, even if I have never actually seen it.'

'You must try to train your mind to be stronger than your emotions. Otherwise, problems only grow bigger and bigger in life,' advised Sabeena. She knew more about life than him, thanks to her tough circumstances. In the Basti, the only thought that mattered was how to survive and earn enough money to buy food. Its residents did not get time to think beyond the battles of their daily survival.

'I do not fully understand many of the things you talk about,' Sabeena continued.

'The world I come from is completely different, brutally wounded by centuries of neglect and criminal discrimination, but I can see what you mean, your feelings, your loneliness. You are a wonderful human being, you are exceptional, you are made for big things.

'But for now, relax a bit, it is not healthy for you to be so stressed for so long. Think of something else for a change. And listen to me as I have more experience than you in such matters—remember, my father thinks I am old enough to be married off!'

The two laughed.

They took a long walk before returning to the Company Garden. 'Let's sit on the steps of the Scouts Hut. I love that space—open, green, plants and shrubs all around,' Sabeena said.

'Fantastic idea,' Vikram responded enthusiastically.

'Oh, this seems to be the firefly season. Look at that side of the shrubs, there's hundreds of them. Fireflies on a moonless night feel as if the stars have descended from the sky to help us forget our pains and miseries, they look like angels from God's kingdom.'

'So, you're a poet too,' Sabeena teased. 'Sing something for me, in my praise.'

'Your eyes are like two moons in the sky and your

face is… as if made of silk from the monsoon clouds… sorry, this is not working, I will try some other time and put it on paper for you.'

'But even these few words are enthralling, coming as they are from….' Sabeena looked wistful. 'Silk from the monsoon clouds…how romantic.'

'Don't read into these lines. These are just words… you know what I mean.'

'I'm worried about my life as I don't know what's in store for me. I have only my Bapu, no one else to fall back on, and all he wants is to marry me off as fast as he can. He says I'm already too old,' Sabeena returned to the real world.

'So far, I could get away from this hell and spend several hours at school. But I'm completing school this month, just like you. There's no college or university in Tundla, which means you either go to Agra or sit at home—or do your Bachelor of Arts degree through correspondence.

'None of this will work for me. It's a dead end for me. I want to study, build a career, but I know I will not be allowed, I will soon be all chained up and thrown into a life I don't want to even think about, let alone live.'

'Don't make me feel more depressed…' mumbled Vikram.

'Do you think I can go against my father on matters like marriage? Two of my friends disappeared after they refused to marry boys of their parents' choice,' she said.

'Nothing will happen to you. All of us, all your friends are here for you. I am, needless to say, always here for you,' Vikram comforted Sabeena, wiping her tears with his blue handkerchief. She quickly took the handkerchief and tucked it away.

Vikram suggested that she continue her studies for a university degree through correspondence or as a private student, which she could do from home. He told her Madhu and he would help her take care of the admission procedure.

'You plan to get admission at St John's College in Agra, right?' asked Sabeena. 'You will be accepted by the college. You're so bright.'

'It's not that easy. St John's College is the best in this part of India, so everybody wants to go there. There are thousands of 'bright boys' like me. I have to prepare for the entrance interview. It's very rigorous there,' said Vikram.

'Have you decided on your subject?'

'Yes. Economics. I will do my 'Bachelors in Economics',' Vikram answered.

'Should I also go for Economics?' Sabeena asked.

'Didn't you want to opt for Psychology?'

'Yeah, but I like Economics too. Economics will help me stay closer to you.'

'What do you mean by that?'

'I mean what I said.'

'But you are close to me already.'

'I said "closer". Do not pretend to be dumb.'

'But we cannot be closer than this,' said Vikram rather dryly, taking Sabeena a little aback.

'Vikram, I love you. Don't you know that?'

Vikram remained quiet.

'I will die without you in my life. I will die,' was all Sabeena could manage to utter before bursting into tears. 'Do you not love me because I am poor and from the Valmiki Dalit community?' asked Sabeena.

'What? What's wrong with you? Is that what you think of me?' Vikram protested.

Sabeena apologised, and Vikram hugged her, saying, 'I don't deserve love from a wonderful girl like you, and you, in any case, deserve someone better than me. I'm not at peace, I'm too restless to even think of having a girlfriend. My goals are different. I feel a huge void in my life—I feel rootless, homeless, sometimes even worthless—I'm looking for a place I can call my own, can anchor my body and soul into, and build a life on.

'A tree that grows without roots is bound to fall and die. In a few years or so or even sooner, financial support from my parents will be gone. I may find a job and survive physically, but my needs are different, my future vision is different—having a job alone will not be enough for me. I want a place to plant myself into. Only a tree with deep roots can grow tall enough to kiss the sky.'

'Anyway, what's this love? In an impoverished and socially orthodox society like Tundla, it's all about marriage, it means almost an instant marriage. And then having kids,' argued Vikram a little irritably.

'I think all your thoughts of love are the result of this massive stress you have been put under by your father. Focus on education, complete your BA first. Build a better life,' he advised.

'In a small town like ours, if you say you love a boy or a girl, families rush to marry you off to that person as soon as they can find a priest to recite the mantras and a caterer to take care of the feast.'

'Don't think I am stupid. I know what I'm talking about. I love you,' said Sabeena, shaking her head. 'You are so self-involved, you know nothing about girls. You don't have a heart.'

Sabeena stood up and walked into the darkness towards her home, wiping rivers of tears with Vikram's blue handkerchief.

Lost, confused, a bit shattered, Vikram sat there wondering, if he had unconsciously allowed her to look at him as a boyfriend, and not just a friend.

'None of my friends ever looked at her as my

girlfriend. I have never behaved with her in that way. I care for her, but she knows my challenges. We are both victims of how societies can treat vulnerable people like her and me. I'm sorry, Sabeena, if I hurt you.'

8

A huge commotion had erupted on the rail tracks around a goods train that had just come to a screeching halt—applying the emergency brakes. The driver, the guard and the crowd were searching for the person, who had jumped in front of the powerful WG steam engine of the Amritsar-Calcutta fast train, carrying wheat from Punjab to the eastern metropolis.

'Where, where? Not here! Look there! No sign of the body, maybe the body has been thrown away, or it got all crushed!' The shouts and alerts from the searching staff, police and volunteers were getting louder and louder.

'It was a girl in a long blue shirt,' cried out the driver of the train.

'Look for the dead body in blue, long blue shirt,' he yelled.

As news spread through Tundla, more people gathered.

'Here she is! But there's no blood!' shouted a

volunteer from under wagon number forty-seven. 'Probably died of shock.'

Dozens of volunteers rushed in that direction, snaking under the wagon. They pulled out the "body" with some difficulty as it had sunk into the depression formed between the two wooden sleepers that were in place to maintain an equal gap between the two rails.

'She's alive!' One of the volunteers gasped. 'Such depressions can emerge when the tracks are not well maintained or are overused. But this is probably what has saved her life,' observed an onlooker, a retired railway engineer.

'There's also a cat, and the girl is alive!'

The rallying voice of other rescuers filled the atmosphere. The onlookers started cheering, calling her lucky. 'How could she survive the weight of such a monstrous locomotive. She has to be a special child.'

'Who is she?' asked a policeman from the Railway Protection Force. He had also arrived with a few armed colleagues.

The volunteers laid the girl on a cloth sheet given by the train driver, so she was comfortable. The cat also jumped out and pawed anxiously at the chest of the girl, nudging closer to her. They sprinkled cold water on the girl's face in an effort to help her stay conscious. Word spread. Soon many from the Quarters arrived at the spot.

'Oh, it's Sabeena! I cannot believe this!' cried Madhu. 'And the cat is Dibbi.' Madhu began to cry. Neha and Vikram had also reached there.

Sabeena was now conscious, but looked dazed and lost.

'Sabeena, what happened, are you okay?' asked Vikram, concerned.

Neha helped Sabeena sip some water that a volunteer brought from a nearby tea shack.

Her hands were trembling. 'What happened? What were you doing jumping on the track?' she asked.

Sabeena was too shocked to speak. Madhu, Vikram and Neha, surrounded her, while the local police debated what to do next. Madhu had dispatched a friend to call Sabeena's father.

Sabeena slowly sat up, hugging Dibbi, and murmuring, 'She saved me, Dibbi saved me.'

Vikram, Madhu and Neha called a cycle rickshaw to take her to the railway's hospital. Everyone assembled requested the police not to register a case of attempted suicide against Sabeena, arguing she was a minor and what had happened was just an accident. Luckily, the police agreed and let her go. No case was registered.

Doctors examined her and declared her alright, but still kept her in the hospital for the next 24 hours. Many friends from the Quarters arrived in to check on her.

Sabeena was happy to see them all. 'I cannot believe

they have all come to see me,' she told Madhu and Neha. 'I thought nobody in the world likes me, none of you care actually about me.' Sabeena was in tears. 'But you do, you all do. Thank you so much.'

Her father arrived, crying like a child. An attending doctor instructed him to stop crying as his wails were disturbing other patients in the ward.

'Blame me, blame me. I am responsible for what happened. I deserve severe punishment, a severe one,' he said, addressing her assembled friends in a low, controlled voice. 'I lost my mind; I deserve severe punishment.'

'But what happened? Why did she try to kill herself? She would not have gone so far without something very serious.' Madhu glanced between Sabeena and her father.

'We had been having arguments for the last few days over my insistence on marrying her off to a boy I know very well, from a good family. She said she didn't want to marry. I lost my cool and slapped her hard many times. She fell on the ground in pain, crying. I had gone mad. Yet, this morning, she made me breakfast and tea as usual, and then left saying she was going to a friend in the neighbourhood. Instead, she jumped in front of the train.' Hari Ram was beating his chest in sorrow.

'Sabeena is the only reason I'm alive. She looks after me like my mother. She loves me so much, and yet, I drove her to end her life. God will never forgive me. My late wife, Sabeena's mother, will never forgive me. I don't deserve to live even a day now!'

Vikram interrupted his lament. 'We all hope you will now stop insisting on her marriage. Do you have any idea how bright and talented she is? She will make you proud, liberate you from poverty and all your miseries. Let her study, set her free.'

Vikram's words meant the world to Sabeena. Madhu told Sabeena's father he would lose her forever if he did not stop trying to marry her off.

'Don't you love her?' questioned Madhu.

'More than my own life, more than God!' Hari Ram answered.

Sabeena's friends asked her father to go home and rest, assuring him they would drop her home the next day after being discharged from the hospital.

'We will discharge her tomorrow at noon,' reassured the attending doctor. 'But please don't stress the patient. Don't ask her so many questions. She's still in shock. We will give her a tranquilliser post dinner for her to get a good night's sleep.'

Sabeena ate some home-cooked snacks that Neha brought, and fell asleep, only to be woken up by the attending doctor, Dr Meena.

He examined her and then sat down next to her. 'What happened? Why did you do what you did?' the doctor asked kindly.

Sabeena's eyes welled up. 'You will not understand,' she answered softly.

'I understand more than you imagine. Yes, I am a doctor now, but I also come from a background similar to yours—poor, marginalised and from the same caste that Mahatma Gandhi named Harijan. My caste has also suffered humiliating and crippling discrimination for centuries. We're in the same boat,' Dr Meena said.

'I have studied medicine from one of the best colleges in the country, and graduated with a distinction. I have a wonderful job and a good salary. But for most, I am still a Harijan, a Dalit, a lower caste Hindu, first—someone who should not be where I am. I have everything, but I struggle to get respect. Most patients still prefer to go to high caste colleagues in the hospital, ignoring me, often right to my face.

'A good education or a good job or good money is no guarantee that these upper caste people will accept you, respect you. First, you have to stand up for yourself. Respect and love yourself,' Dr Meena said gently.

'Your friends are more open-minded. They are of an age when they can practice their idealism.'

Sabeena found that tears were rolling down her cheeks. The doctor patted her head. 'Take rest. I will be around here.'

Earlier in the afternoon the rain had been unusually heavy. The football ground was wet and smelled sweet.

Two eucalyptus trees at the left corner of the ground swayed as if in celebration of the downpour. The concrete tennis courts were crowded with kids on their colourful tricycles and mini bicycles, with their mothers watching them. A pandemonium of parrots chased each other in the fresh blue sky. Cuckoos, parked safely on the high branches of the majestic neem tree, sung sweetly.

'This is so refreshing,' said Sabeena, joining Vikram, Neha and Madhu.

'Happy to see you happy, Sabeena,' said Madhu.

'Thank you all so very much for everything,' she replied.

'Thank you also for forgiving me for my stupidity. I had some terrible few weeks. I felt I was getting sucked into a dark, never-ending tunnel to nowhere. I felt robbed of all hope, all energy. My father's unrelenting pressure on me to agree to marry the boy he had already chosen only made matters worse.

'I lost it all when he slapped me so hard repeatedly that I fell on the ground, almost unconscious. I picked up Dibbi—who would have looked after her if I was gone? I left home the next morning determined to reach the Kingdom of God, and never return to this hell. I wanted to be free and liberated.'

Vikram, Madhu and Neha listened to her in complete silence, not interrupting her or breaking the flow of her emotions.

'I wore a blue shirt because I also like blue, just like a friend I know well,' Sabeena said, prompting Neha to look at her brother questioningly.

'On reaching the rail tracks, I immediately noticed a goods train speeding from the Delhi side. As soon as the steam engine drew close, I jumped in front of it. Dibbi panicked and flattened herself on the ground, facing the train. She slid into a small cavity between the rails and the sleepers. I followed her, falling into the same space between the two rails and sleepers.'

She sighed. 'Next, I found myself praying to God to save Dibbi and me as the first boiling hot locomotive thundered over me with a loud screech. My eyes were shut, but I could count the wagons from the sound of their wheels…and then the train stopped. I think it was then that I became unconscious. I had come to die, but as I jumped in front of the train I realised, I wanted to live.'

'It's a sin to even entertain such a thought. You should have come to us, to any one of us. Obviously, you had given up on us, you had concluded we were not your friends,' Vikram said, looking at her, his expression a mix of concern, and barely restrained anger.

'I had lost my mind. But from now on, I will work to be a stronger person.'

Madhu and Neha comforted Sabeena, saying they understood her vulnerabilities and state of mind, but still, to go to the extent that she did was not alright.

That night, Sabeena could not sleep. The suicide attempt had jolted every sense in her body and mind. She felt as if she had suddenly aged. It was disturbing. The immediate world around her looked tougher than ever before. She felt lonelier than ever before, and yet stronger at the same time.

Realisation dawned on Sabeena that she had to fight her battles alone. The friends in the Quarters were a great help, but she had discovered that their support would be based on what they thought was good for her and not what she thought would be best for her or what she wanted.

Deep down, Hari Ram disapproved of all her friends and the influence they had on her. He would have been happiest if she had not acquired and developed what he thought were dangerous strains of thoughts.

He could be heard saying to his friends, '*Meri ladki hath se nikal gayee…* My daughter has slipped out of my control.'

'You are doing fine. No more medicines, but avoid any stress and hard work for the next two weeks and come back to me anytime,' said Dr Meena, when Sabeena went back to him for a review check as prescribed.

'Doctor, I'm much lower than you even within the low Dalit caste pyramid. Did you mean that no matter how hard I work in getting higher education, my fate will remain the same? I will still remain a person punished to live on margins and in exploitation?' Sabeena asked.

'Besides, life for a woman is always a hundred times harder than for a man.'

'Social change can take a long time to be implemented. Still, you must get the best education, earn well and save money and learn to fight for your rights whenever necessary. We must all fight for justice. The caste system is an evil and must be dismantled. Let us believe in ourselves and fight.' Dr Meena advised her.

'Live with your head held high. There's no need to live in shame. You are just as worthy as anyone from the so-called higher castes.'

Sabeena went on to score a Distinction in her 12th standard examination. Her father celebrated the day by distributing sweets throughout the Basti. Vikram and Madhu also managed a First Division.

Sabeena decided to pursue a BA in Economics from Agra University, as a private student, which meant she did not have to attend any college regularly. Vikram and Madhu were both lucky to crack the entrance test to enter St John's College at Agra. Some of their cricket team friends joined colleges in Aligarh and Firozabad, for Bachelors of Commerce and Science degrees. Others left Tundla for distant universities to pursue engineering. Two joined a prominent medical college in Kanpur.

The groups of friends Vikram and Sabeena were part of had broken up—gone distances. They would be friends, but it would never be the same again. In fact, their life would never be the same again. Vikram's ache for a nest, a place he could call his own, a home, now acquired a new level of vigour.

9

Going from Tundla to St John's College at Agra, the nearest city, barely eighteen kilometres away, was still a huge leap for Vikram. The buzzing city was home to colleges, cinemas, hotels, industries, the iconic Red Fort, and, most importantly, the Taj Mahal. The change was a welcome shock for Vikram. He loved it.

The new horizons felt endless—places, people, smells, experiences. On his very first day, Vikram took a long boat ride on the river Yamuna from the Red Fort. Later, Madhu and he visited the Taj Mahal. They followed up their visit with a glass of cold coffee at the fancy Capri restaurant, not far from their college. The first week was the orientation week, giving students time to familiarise themselves with fellow freshers and explore the campus facilities. Vikram had plenty of free time to soak it all in.

St John's College, established in 1850, had produced

a President of India, several ministers and governors, scientists, writers and distinguished experts across various fields, over more than a century. Being accepted there as a student was considered recognition of one's merits—such was the college's reputation across northern India. Vikram was in awe of the college from day one.

The morning assembly in the intricate Main Hall was always an experience. Students were ushered in and asked to take their seats before the faculty entered in a procession from the entrance gate, led by the principal in his long, black don robe. He would call on everyone to rise, read a prayer, make some practical announcements, and then dismiss the assembly. Vikram loved it, saying it instilled discipline and order.

Madhu hated it, grumbling, 'It's like we're back in kindergarten.'

Most of students came from affluent families, judging by their clothes and mannerisms. Vikram and Madhu often wondered if they had made the right decision by joining an institution, probably not meant for the "Tundla-type".

'Many of them are loaded with money, arrogant and snooty,' Madhu would often complain.

'Let's just focus on our studies,' Vikram would comfort her.

He owned only two pairs of faded trousers and shirts for college and wore a simple pair of rubber slippers. About forty percent of the students were girls, many of them turning up in style.

Every day, they experienced a fresh shock. 'We are in an ocean now, out from our little pond. We have to learn to live and survive here—in this big college, in this big city. It's exciting, but also frightening. I feel small and insignificant, even vulnerable,' Vikram would often tell Madhu.

'It's a bit like Sabeena's situation. Being here, helps me understand her better.'

'Sometimes I think you have probably fallen in love with Sabeena. Be brave and admit it,' Madhu teased him.

'Stop it,' he protested.

'You are now almost an adult. *Pyar vyar karo, maze lo*. Fall in love, make love, have fun!' Madhu continued. He laughed her words off.

Vikram boarded a train in the morning to Agra, rushed to the college from the station, attended classes, and then boarded an evening train back to Tundla. The train journey took about an hour, but was often prolonged by delays.

Vikram hated commuting, because it cut short his time in the library, and more importantly, his time to participate in extracurricular activities, like debates and discussions on current topics. Staying in the college's students' hostel was not an option—his parents could not afford the high fees. The daily commute did not cost anything as children from the railways were entitled to free travel in trains.

Bullying of the studious boys and harassment of good-looking girls on the trains was common and widespread. Most of the bullies belonged to ill-reputed colleges. Quitting was not an option, so Vikram soon developed his own techniques to deal with them. As part of this strategy, he would sit with the roughies in the train and share jokes and funny anecdotes with them. Vikram realised that this boosted their self-image and in return they listened to him, often seeking his advice and tips on how to do well in studies.

Confident of the support he had built among the roughies, Vikram took a bold stand, three months into his commuter life. When a boy tried to kiss Madhu, Vikram thrashed him, and forced him to jump off the train just as it had started to pull away from the platform. Madhu was stunned; she could not believe her eyes. By the next morning, the entire Quarters were buzzing with talk of Vikram's transformation into a macho man.

He had come a long way in a short time. The college, the daily commute, and the city of Agra had shaped him—from a dreamer to a survivor. Vikram was evolving rapidly, to the delight of his family. The new world fascinated him. He was developing a sense of taste and appreciation of quality. He noticed class and finesse in everything done at St John's—whether it was producing a prospectus, drafting a notice or organising an event—everything was executed with the highest standards.

Yet, deep inside he remained restless.

'I'm still as restless as ever searching for my moorings—for a place I can truly call home, my *mitti*. But I suppose I'm more mature, better equipped to express myself—thanks to St John's College! This place is the reason for this transformation in me; the change I experience in myself every day. I'm so utterly happy to be learning so much here,' he told his sister Neha, when he took her to Agra to show her around his college. Madhu and Sabeena were with them too.

'Such a magnificent building, you are so lucky, Vikram,' said Sabeena.

'Do you and Vikram still feel that inferiority complex?' Neha asked Madhu.

'It's getting better,' Madhu replied, 'We still don't feel as if we belong, but we are getting there,' added Vikram.

'I think I will also try for this college after school,' Neha announced. Sabeena looked lost and withdrawn.

St John's College did boast some of the best college buildings in northern India, built in red sandstone in the Indo-Saracenic architectural style, adorned with elaborate features and intricate artwork.

'There's something in the air of this college that

transforms you,' Vikram sighed, as they walked around. It's like the ancient Indian universities of Nalanda and Takshila—or Oxford and Harvard in the West.'

They stopped at the Central Library, located at the far end of the sprawling campus, before walking back to the main building via the famous Love Lane—a favourite haunt of young lovers, canopied by fragrant trees and shrubs, where privacy and space were fiercely respected. The Lane had become an institution in itself, with its own lores and legends. It was home to kingfishers, bulbuls, owls, sunbirds, cuckoos and even peacocks.

Many couples returned here regularly, to the spot they had first met where their love blossomed. The Lane dipped slightly in the middle before rising again, flanked by a dense forest of flowers on both sides. Sabeena enchanted, named it the "Valley of Flowers".

'I didn't know they facilitate falling in love here as well,' Neha remarked, glancing at Sabeena.

Sabeena lost in thought, felt deeply grateful for the chance to visit such a remarkable institution. She knew she too could have been a student here—had she been luckier. Sensing what was going through her mind, Neha warmly hugged her.

Later, they decided to watch a Bollywood movie at the Rajshree Theatre. Watching the latest movie in a modern and fully air-conditioned hall was a first for all of them. Afterwards, they walked down to the station to catch the evening train back home, where their anxious families were waiting.

Sabeena shared the day's experience with Dibbi before turning affectionately to her father.

He looked at her coldly. 'Why do you keep talking about things that are not in your fate?'

Taken aback, Sabeena reacted dismissively, 'I don't care about fate…All I know is, I enjoyed the day and now you have to listen to my tales. I'm so happy, can't you see?'

Her father gave in with a reluctant smile, 'Okay, go on, let me join you in what you call a day of joy.'

Later that night, Sabeena decided to write a note of thanks to Vikram:

My dear Vikram,
Many thanks for including me in the group that toured your beautiful college today. I didn't know such institutions even existed. I also discovered many new sides and shades of the world and of you—you are a wonderful man, kind and so mature. Neha and Madhu were also so kind to me. Stay focused on your studies.

My best wishes, always.
Sabeena.

She read the letter aloud to Dibbi, kissed it several times, and then suddenly dropped it into the embers of her coal-fired kitchen stove. She cried uncontrollably, with Dibbi held tightly in her arms, as the letter turned into a fireball, and then dust. She wept the entire night in her bed.

Agra was not a metropolis like Bombay or Calcutta. It was often dismissed by urban connoisseurs as a "sleepy" provincial city in the dusty plains of northern India, but for someone from a small, isolated place like Tundla, it felt as grand as London or Tokyo. An educational hub, the city attracted students from far-off countries—Iran, Iraq, Afghanistan and Africa. Thanks to the Taj Mahal, thousands of visitors from all parts of the world descended on it every day, eager to get photographed with one of the Seven Wonders of the World.

Vikram wanted to tap into everything good the city had to offer. He developed a deep interest in Mughal history and architecture, attending a workshop on the subject organised by the Archaeological Survey of India. Madhu often borrowed books on history from different libraries around the city and passed them on to him.

Winters were always special. Students assembled in small groups on the lush green lawns in front of the college's main building, soaking in the afternoon sun, chatting and gossiping.

During one such gathering Vikram approached Professor Reid Williams, who was returning to his department, after lunch at his campus residence, holding some books and a copy of a folded newspaper.

'Could I borrow the newspaper for the day, sir, once you're are finished with it sir?' Vikram asked.

'This paper—*The Observer*, you know about this newspaper?' the professor replied, surprised.

'I listen to the BBC World Service regularly. They often quote it in their stories.' Vikram said.

The professor smiled. 'Of course, come and collect it from my residence, tomorrow.'

Vikram was thrilled. '*The Observer!* From London!'

'Why are you so happy? It's just a newspaper,' Madhu said, puzzled.

'This paper is a window to the world.'

The next day, Vikram reached Professor Williams's bungalow at the appointed time. The professor invited him into the front lawn. Mrs Williams soon joined them, with a tray of cookies and tea.

'Thank you both very much. I feel honoured,' Vikram murmured, choosing his words carefully—he wanted to make the best possible impression on his hosts.

'We are here from Edinburgh on a five-year assignment. This paper helps me stay in touch with developments back in the United Kingdom and the rest of the world,' said Professor Williams, handing over the copy of *The Observer*.

'Thank you,' said Vikram. 'I will return it tomorrow.'

'Read and enjoy it. Return it once you have gone through it,' said the professor. 'You can borrow it from us every week.'

They spoke about classes and what Vikram did in his free time. Afterwards, Vikram thanked them and left to catch his train home, but he was so desperately curious that he started flipping through the newspaper while walking towards the nearest railway station. He was overwhelmed by the developments of the day—getting to know a prominent professor of the college, having tea with him, holding a copy of an international newspaper in his hands.

Vikram spent the entire night reading, *The Observer* and making notes. He was particularly drawn to a feature article on the top UK universities, like Oxford, Cambridge and St Andrews. Another feature story, on the ongoing cold war between the United States and the Union of Soviet Socialist Republic fascinated him. He also read and made notes on a long piece on how the refugees from some war-torn countries in Africa were attempting to enter Britain and Europe.

The following day, Vikram borrowed two books on the state of African refugees in Europe, including one about how Uganda's President Idi Amin forced over 80,000 Indians settled in the African country to leave within 90 days, dooming them to a life of hopelessness and economic, cultural, and social poverty. Many sought refuge in Britain and other West European countries.

Vikram read the two books intensely, drawing parallels with his own life and the fate of his family. Inspired, he penned a short piece of fiction for his college magazine. It was the story of a Ugandan Gujarati boy, forced to relocate from Kampala to a small village near York in England. The boy's family once owners of a grand bungalow and a fleet of chauffeur driven cars, were reduced to working-class migrants in England, a foreign land.

He also read extensively about how Africans were taken to the United States as slaves, and what their social and economic status was now. He explored the histories of poor, illiterate Indians, mostly from Bihar, fraudulently taken to Fiji, Mauritius, South America and the Caribbean to work as bonded labour.

He kept digging into his college's rich library resources for books on refugees, slavery, exploitation, cultural suffering and marginalisation. Some of these discussed the fates of Indians who had died during the First and Second World Wars while fighting for Britain, a colonial power. The more he read, the more he realised everything his parents, especially his father, had gone through, and what he himself was going through.

Vikram also felt grateful that he had spoken to Professor Williams, and continued to talk to him about whatever he was reading at the moment. Professor Williams had completed his doctorate in English Literature from the University of Oxford and his Master's from the University of St Andrews in Scotland. He was a teacher in the true sense of the word, always helping whoever sought him out, conducting free workshops in English language proficiency, and mentoring the debating and dramatics societies. He was an accomplished theatre artist himself.

As the countdown to the end of their first year at St John's began, Vikram hesitantly asked Professor Williams if it would be too unrealistic for a person of his economic and social background to think of applying for a Master's from the University of Oxford.

'Do you think I'm dreaming too big?' he asked the professor candidly.

The professor considered him for a moment. 'You still have time. Get back to me in October, after the Dussehra festival vacation.'

Vikram was thrilled—the professor was not dismissive. He had mentally prepared to be laughed off or even ridiculed for entertaining such a thought.

In fact, Professor Williams had already been thinking of how he could support Vikram. He told Vikram he had come a very long way intellectually and in all-round development. He should feel proud of his progress.

'But it is a long road ahead, and your journey has only just begun.'

10

Hari Ram invited only Vikram, Neha, and Madhu from the Quarters to the wedding ceremony of his daughter.

The invitation read:

Hari Ram invites you on the auspicious occasion of the wedding of his beloved daughter Aleena alias Sabeena with Hussein Bhisti, son of Amir Bhisti, on September 7, at the Peepal Courtyard, Valmiki Basti, Tundla.

Please join us for lunch after the ceremony.

The news came as a huge shock to her friends and well-wishers in the Quarters.

'This is criminal, this is injustice,' Madhu reacted, crying.

'Her father is a selfish crank!' Neha was angry too. 'He just wants to get rid of her, he is so heartless!'

The trio huddled together. Vikram remained silent,

speechless and unsure about what to do.

Lakshmi explained that marriage at this age, especially for girls, was common. 'Sometimes people, both lower and upper castes, marry off their daughters even younger, which is against the law, but they do. Sabeena is lucky, she is over eighteen now. I'm sure most of her friends in the Basti must have already been married off by now. Many consider having a daughter a burden, a liability, and they want to unburden themselves as soon as possible.'

Sabeena had met Vikram twice in the past fortnight to alert him of her father's ultimatum to either agree to the marriage, or live with his suicide on her conscience. Hari Ram had told her that he was dying of lung cancer and had only a few months to live, and he wanted to see her married off before he was gone.

'I will be able to die peacefully once you are married, settled and secure at your husband's home. I have chosen a gem of a boy for you—handsome and well employed,' he kept repeating to Sabeena.

'And I have to fulfil the commitment I made to your parent, the commitment that I would hand you over to a good Muslim Bhisti boy in marriage.'

She had protested and pleaded a million times. 'I did everything I could—cried, pleaded, prayed and even threatened another attempt at suicide, but nothing worked,' she lamented. 'Baba is sick and broken. I cannot see him die disappointed in front of my eyes. I love him. He is my father.'

She had continued, 'Vikram, I want to study, achieve something in life. I have dreams for me, for my father. I know I am blessed with a good mind, but my father cannot see all this. I don't blame him, he has his own limitations, and society has treated him so badly that he does not trust anybody. He behaves like a dead man walking, no dreams, no ambitions.'

'Madhu, Neha, I don't think we can do much. It's heartbreaking, but we cannot intervene—her father and the others in the Basti will misunderstand us, putting her in deeper trouble,' Vikram said, breaking his silence. 'Let's support her, but not intervene. She has to fight this battle herself.'

The two girls kept quiet, but Neha could not hold herself together any longer. She exploded, 'You boys can never understand girls, their emotions, or their heart!'

Madhu, crying, added, 'We could have gone and talked to her mother had she been alive. It's no point talking to her father.'

Madhu and Neha still decided to go and meet Hari Ram.

The Basti was as noisy, dirty and chaotic as ever. Groups of men were idling at every corner. All eyes turned on Madhu and Neha as they walked through the lanes to Sabeena's shanty.

Sabeena responded to the knock at the door. Pleasantly surprised, she hugged them tight and burst into tears, before gesturing for them to come in and sit down on. She called her father, who was taking a nap inside. Hari Ram was reluctant to come out, but he did after Sabeena argued that it would be rude not to meet their guests.

'We look forward to welcoming you at the wedding ceremony. Please do join us,' said Hari Ram.

'We gather you have lung cancer. Did you consult Dr Gupta? We could ask him to examine you if you want,' Madhu said. 'He is a brilliant doctor, the best in town.'

'We have a doctor in the Basti. He told me that I have cancer and I will be gone soon. He is good. His father was also a doctor,' Hari Ram said.

'But is he a qualified one?' Neha asked.

'Yes, he was trained by his father, who was also a doctor. Everyone in the Basti goes to him. We cannot afford these English doctors.'

'You mean allopathic doctors,' Neha sought to clarify.

'Yes, these doctors who prescribe foreign medicines.'

'But how could a doctor who is not trained conclude you were dying of lung cancer?' Madhu argued gently.

'Just by reading my pulse, my face, he can tell the state of my health. He is brilliant and very inexpensive,' Hari Ram explained, 'but do not worry about my health…I'm done with this life anyway. I'm not important. Sabeena is my life. My life is all about my daughter and her safe future. I'm constantly worried about her future.'

'We wish you good health and a long life. Our concern was if you could reconsider and postpone Sabeena's marriage until she has earned her degree,' Madhu said, holding Sabeena's hand.

'The boy's family will not wait. I will also be soon gone because of the cancer. I have no time. It is all done. The invitations have gone.' Hari Ram raised his hands up in a gesture of dismissal. 'I plead with you Quarters folks not to interfere in our affairs.' He stood up and haltingly walked away to complete his nap.

The three girls cried together in despair and helplessness. Neha and Madhu left for home, walking numbly.

Sabeena also left home for a long walk. She knew her fate was now sealed.

The Quarters were abuzz organising the annual Harshringar festival. The night jasmine was in full bloom; the flowers were addictively fragrant and beautiful, with lovely white petals and an orange centre.

The flower's season was brief, from late August to October. The buds opened at dusk and dropped to the ground before sunrise. Some poets called Harshringar a flower of sorrow, but many in India identified the flower with joy and good luck, and the beginning of winter. Revered as a divine flower by Hindus, it was offered in devotion to Gods in the temple.

Almost every home in the Quarters had at least one plant of Harshringar. Vikram had five, Madhu had six. Sabeena, a regular at the festival, had two. On the festival day, the boys and girls of the quarters had decided to plant two hundred saplings in different parts of Tundla.

The Quarters was decorated with sparklers, colourful paper flags, and banners. The residents had pooled money to hire a music system, a canopy, snacks and beverages to enjoy the evening festivities. After a small prayer for a long and happy life for all Harshringars in the world, volunteers who had gone around to plant the saplings shared their reports and experiences, followed by a small lecture by an expert botanist from Agra.

Once the formalities concluded, the boys and girls played Bollywood songs on the music system. Soon, everyone began to dance—uncles, aunts and even the grand uncles and aunts joined in. The quarters were transformed into a carnival. It was late in the evening and the entire place was soaked in colour, joy and laughter.

Vikram and Madhu, the driving forces behind

the event, were ecstatic.

Madhu and Neha had just finished their last samosa and fresh lime water when a young boy came running towards them and started pulling them out of the canopy, screaming, 'Help! Sabeena has jumped into the well! She is drowning!'

The girls panicked and shouted for someone to shut down the loud music system, calling everyone to follow them. Soon almost the entire crowd gathered around the *Acchut Kuan.*

Two teenaged boys from the Basti jumped into the well in an attempt to rescue Sabeena, while others started lowering two sets of ropes into the well. It was dark, but over a dozen battery torch lights appeared in no time from the Quarters, lighting up the well. The rescuers were experts in cleaning water tanks, and were at home even in the depth of the well. They were holding Sabeena on their shoulders as she was unconscious, while tying the ropes together to create a small basket to bring all three of them up to safety. The operation lasted over thirty minutes.

Hari Ram sat on the parapet by the well, shocked and silent.

When Sabeena was on solid ground, Madhu and Neha placed two towels around her, trying to dry her, while Vikram called a cycle rickshaw to take her to Dr Ghosh's clinic in town. Sabeena had failed in another attempt to end her life—to escape a forced marriage.

Hari Ram discussed the matter with an informal body of the influential figures of the Basti, who unanimously advised that now it was even more important to marry her off quickly.

'The wedding ceremony will happen as scheduled on 7 September.'

Madhu and Neha cried incessantly. Madhu had to be taken to the hospital at midnight as she developed shivers and a fever because of the emotional stress.

The wedding ceremony was an extremely simple affair. A worn-out tent was pitched at an open space near the *peepal* tree, with a cheap carpet on the floor for the guests to sit on. The groom, Hussein Bhisti, dark and already balding, looked about forty years old. He arrived with a procession of twenty-five relatives and friends. They were welcomed with sherbet by Hari Ram, his friends and the local residents.

The gathering was small—only fifty men, women and children. Sabeena's father could not afford to host any more guests.

Vikram had chosen not to attend.

Neha and Madhu were helping Sabeena get ready.

Sabeena looked like an apsara, despite her ordinary wedding dress and imitation jewellery.

'Our Sabeena looks like a princess. She's easily one

of the most beautiful girls in the world,' Madhu, kept repeating, awestruck by her friend's beauty.

The bride, however, remained lifeless. Madhu and Neha felt as if they had dressed up a statue.

The girls from the Quarters walked the bride from her home to the wedding venue, where the rituals were conducted in the traditional Muslim way. Sabeena did everything that she was asked to, including giving her consent for the marriage when asked by the *maulvi*. The priest pronounced Hussein and Sabeena as husband and wife. The customary congratulations followed, acknowledged by the bride with an icy silence.

Hari Ram looked relaxed, now. He went around greeting everyone, asking them to bless his daughter, and gesturing them to move where lunch had been served.

Lunch was not lavish: two vegetable dishes, chicken in spicy curry, and puris. Only one sweet was served. That was all Sabeena's father could afford. The boy's side had asked for three non-vegetarian dishes, including lamb curry. Friends in the Basti had asked for pork in tomato curry, which Hari Ram dismissed, arguing that serving pork at a Muslim wedding was not done.

Madhu and Neha did not eat as a sign of protest.

Sabeena requested them to secretly take her to the Hanuman temple to pray briefly. She offered prayers for fifteen minutes, while rivers of tears pooled over her roughly rouged cheeks. She was in unbearable pain.

Sabeena handed her friends a letter addressed to Vikram, which read:

Dear Vikram,
I died a long time ago. They have married off my body today, not me. I could not resist any longer as I had lost all will to live. I hope to meet you as a life partner in my next birth. Stay well and may God help you in realising all your ambitions and dreams.

I love you.
Sabeena.

The note did not surprise Madhu or Neha. They knew about her love for Vikram.

Hari Ram was searching for his daughter nervously as the three girls returned to the wedding venue. Soon Hussein invited Sabeena to board the waiting cycle rickshaw. Hari Ram and everyone assembled from the bride's side were in tears as they bade her goodbye. Madhu and Neha cried the most.

Sabeena had spent all her life in a house where she was the boss, ever since she was old enough to make tea for her father. Hussein's house was very crowded, dirtier, and more impoverished than hers.

'Is this my father's definition of a well-off boy, a good family?' Sabeena lamented in her mind.

Her husband introduced her to all his family members and assembled relatives.

At night, she was shown a dingy space in a corner of a larger room, where the newlyweds would spend their first night. Sabeena asked for a broom and a bucket of water and spent an hour cleaning the room.

The girls in Hussein's family looked at her surprised and giggled, 'She wants to enjoy her honeymoon in clean comfort.'

The husband arrived soon after, and was surprised at the transformation of the room. Sabeena took him even further by surprise, and launched into a brief monologue, sharing the reasons she agreed to this marriage, and making it clear they would not be husband and wife in the traditional sense.

'I agreed to this marriage because I was under huge pressure from my father. He threatened to kill himself and I didn't want to lose my dear father. So, I had no option but to agree.' Sabeena told Hussein, requesting him to take the bed. She said, she would sleep on the floor.

'We are not husband and wife in this room. You should never ever try to touch me. I am not yours.'

Hussein did not know how to react. He sat stunned.

He had never met a girl so articulate, smart and astute. In his job as a cleaner in the municipality in a nearby town, he had no chance to meet girls, let alone one as educated and enlightened as Sabeena. She also requested him to call her by her name, Sabeena, not by her Muslim name.

'You are not like other women—I mean, not like my sisters or cousins,' he said at last.

'You are free to marry again. Ask your father to arrange another marriage for you. She can be your wife in bed. I will have no issue with that,' Sabeena told a shocked Hussein.

'Another wife? You must be joking!' he said, 'Take your time. Everything will be fine. You must be anxious. It is our first night, you can take as much time as you need.'

'No, no, I was very clear from the beginning. You didn't come to meet me. Otherwise, I would have told you all this before the marriage.'

A few weeks later, Hussein took a reluctant Sabeena to see the Taj Mahal. He narrated the story of the deep love Emperor Shah Jahan had for his wife Mumtaz Mahal and how he built the monument in her memory, hoping to gain Sabeena's love.

'I know the story,' she rebuffed him.

He tried to hold her hand as they walked to the main entrance of the Mahal, but she shook his hand off with a stern warning never to try this again. They did not exchange a word for the next two weeks.

Sabeena was always polite and proper with everyone in Hussein's family and their neighbours. She would do all the required household work and spent most of her spare time studying.

Six months into his marriage with Sabeena, Hussein married again—this time to a cousin, who did not live far from their house.

Sabeena had brought prestige to Hussein and his family among the relatives and neighbours. But she was growing deeply unhappy and wanted to get away from all of this. Yet she did not want to do anything that would hurt her father. Hari Ram's health was failing fast. Sabeena also noticed that Hussein, a chain smoker, coughed a lot. She asked his new wife to take him to the hospital for a thorough medical check.

The two women took Hussein for a medical checkup to a hospital in Firozabad. After an X-ray and thorough tests, the doctor diagnosed that Hussein was suffering from an advanced stage of a serious infectious disease in his lungs.

He told him to isolate himself from everyone in the family for a year or two, or until he had recovered completely.

'Stay away from your wife too, otherwise, she will also contract it,' the doctor ordered.

Sabeena was apathetic and did not react at all. But Hussein and his second wife were shattered. Life got tougher for everyone. And most of all, for Sabeena.

11

Vikram had earned a good name for himself in college. He was recognised as a person with many strong, original ideas, thanks to his regular contribution of articles to local and national newspapers. His article, *'Why Agra Needs a New University',* brought him into the limelight across all the colleges in the city.

He focused entirely on his studies, often leaving the college library late in the evening. His mission was to achieve the highest rank in the final examinations.

Professor Reid Williams invited Vikram home for a working lunch. Some sandwiches and boiled potatoes were served at the table. A large white envelope lay on a side table, with the words *Oxford Institute of New Economics and Finance* written prominently on the top.

'Apply for this Institute's Master programme. Take this application form, study it very carefully and come back to me on Saturday. I will try my best to help you get in there and apply for a scholarship,' Professor Williams said, handing over the envelope to Vikram.

'Let's have lunch, I hope you like blue cheese sandwiches.'

Vikram, excited by the application, and a little bemused about the lunch, said, 'Sir, I have never had cheese in my life, let alone blue cheese.'

The lunch over, Vikram touched the Professor's feet. 'Sir, I am so grateful to you.'

'I am just doing my job, helping a bright student.'

Vikram was on cloud nine. After lunch, he did not return to the library as planned. He rushed home to share the news with his family, and with Madhu. The family burst into loud cheers as Vikram waved the white envelope.

'Oxford, what a dream!' declared a jubilant Neha. Their parents struggled to hold back their tears.

His mother kept repeating, 'God bless you. 'A brutally displaced family's son was being considered for Oxford! God has his own way of blessing us.'

Vikram knocked at Madhu's door with the news too. Exultant, Madhu hugged Vikram tight, 'This is wonderful. You will get in; you will definitely get in.'

She walked back with Vikram to the Sarhadi household, where she was offered some *halwa*.

'Let's keep this between us until Vikram has an acceptance letter in hand,' insisted Sudarshan

Sarhadi. Everyone nodded in agreement to keep it secret, for the time being.

But Madhu's mother, a notorious gossip, had overheard her daughter and Vikram talking. By the next day, everyone had heard the news in the Quarters.

Annoyed, and embarrassed, Madhu confronted her mother for sharing it prematurely and for being envious of the boy next door.

'Why should I be happy for this uncultured boy?' her mother snapped. 'But I want Oxford to accept him so that he's gone from here, hopefully forever. This boy has had such a bad influence on my innocent daughter, good riddance. He has corrupted all the girls in the Quarters.'

St John's College had organised an optional two-week workshop for students on a first-come, first-served basis to further sharpen their English language and conversation skills, as well as their general manners and etiquette. Vikram was the first one to register, Madhu the second. The duo was among the most enthusiastic participants.

Vikram was confident that Oxford would accept him. In the meantime, he focussed on winning accolades for the college in inter-university debates and writing competitions, and was also awarded for his active engagement in extracurriculars.

Vikram loved his annual Christmas holidays—the

festive mood, cold nights, foggy days—enjoying the long walks, sometimes holding a piping hot cup of tea. Madhu, who often joined him—was enthralled by the romantic weather and often burst into Bollywood love melodies, while out on these walks.

'You are not romantic; you are just shameless. How can you sing a love song in a public space, and that too while walking with a guy who's not even remotely your lover?' he chastened Madhu once, as they left for a walk post-dinner, amidst dense fog.

'You can sing a love song without thinking of anybody specific,' Madhu rebutted, grabbing Vikram's arm and holding it tight.

She commented about how cold the night was. 'You are such a warm and dependable friend. I would have loved having a disciplined and kind husband like you, but someone funny, a romantic like me—not boring like you.'

Vikram laughed.

'You don't have to love somebody to sing a love song—and you don't have to love that person to make love to him. We can make love without being in love,' Madhu told Vikram teasingly.

College reopened to an elaborate New Year Mela on the main ground. The mood was festive, with students enjoying games and food at various stalls that the first-year students had organised. The Girls Association had put up a stall selling what they called Roman Pizza, unheard of in the city, yet it attracted the longest queue. Madhu and Vikram waited for over an hour for their turn, but it was worth the wait as they loved the delicacy. The mela went on till late in the evening and Vikram had a great time with his friends.

In February, life started slowing down in the college as students switched into intense study mode, preparing for their examinations.

One Friday evening in February, marked one of the most important events in Vikram's life—his acceptance into Oxford, with a full scholarship. He kissed the Letter of Acceptance repeatedly, awaiting him when he reached home from college.

Celebrations broke out. A large basket of sweets was ordered. The residents from the Quarters poured in to greet the Sarhadis and enjoy the sweets. Madhu supervised all the arrangements. Sabeena was the last one to appear, carrying a small box of sweet dumplings for Vikram. She insisted on feeding him the dumplings herself. Madhu and Neha cheered and clapped as she fed Vikram. Sabeena wore a joyful face for the occasion, but beneath she looked quite exhausted and withdrawn. Nobody asked her any questions. She stayed for only ten minutes. Neha noticed a man had escorted her, but she could not recognise him.

In the end of February, Vikram won the *Student*

of the Year award. He also won the *Top Student in Economics* award. Madhu was voted *Best Student* in her class. Vikram's hard work paid off even further when he topped the college in his Final Year Examination. Madhu topped in her class.

But Sabeena outshone them all; despite being a private student, she topped the University, which had over 100 colleges affiliated to it, scoring two percent more marks than Vikram. Sabeena's photograph appeared across local media, with her favourite quote, *'Where there is a will, there is a way'* splashed across headlines. The area's largest selling Hindi daily carried her story in full detail—how she managed to score the top rank despite her struggles and the massive challenges she faced.

'I realised I had to study hard to get out of the darkness. I would study until 3 or 4 am on most days. The girls from the Quarters would send me any books I needed—that was so kind of them. I knew only a good rank in the examination would be able to rescue me.'

She was an instant inspiration for many and, unsurprisingly, the talk of many towns in the Agra region.

Madhu, Neha and Vikram invited Sabeena to a restaurant near St John's to celebrate the occasion. She agreed on the condition that she would be picked up as well as dropped back. They travelled by train to Agra, touring the college campus one last time, before heading to the restaurant for lunch. They ordered piping hot *chholey-bhature*, with accompaniments of onions, pickled carrots, mango chutney and fresh curd. Sabeena looked tense, but tried her best to enjoy the occasion and the food.

Madhu noticed an injury mark on the left side of her neck and whispered, asking if everything was okay. Sabeena kept quiet, taking her handkerchief out from her bag in an effort to stop a tear drop that was about to slip down her cheek.

'Excuse me,' she said, and stood up to go to the washroom.

'I think she's being abused,' Madhu muttered as they waited for her to rejoin.

'You both should talk to her,' Vikram said.

'Yes, we shall,' Neha answered.

Madhu and Neha insisted on picking up the bill. The four of them walked down to the train station.

Vikram deliberately walked slightly ahead so that the three girls could talk. Sabeena broke down and confided that her husband and his family physically and mentally abused her. 'Only yesterday my husband tried to strangle me with a leather belt, but he gave up after I fought back. I don't think I am safe there,' Sabeena said, wiping her tears.

'My husband didn't want me to come out today, but I told him he had no right to stop me,' Sabeena continued, 'My life is hell.'

Madhu quipped, 'These men, they all are the same. Marriage is such a suffocating, rotten institution.'

Neha reacted more calmly, 'Don't generalise. There are good men and there are bad men. Similarly, there are good women and there are bad women. It's about good people and bad people. Her husband is a bad person.'

'Madhu, you need to look after and protect Sabeena when I go to Oxford,' Vikram said to Madhu on the train back.

'Don't worry about me,' Sabeena sighed.

Madhu took Sabeena's hand in hers, saying, 'Never worry. I will not let that bastard harm you. Neha and I will work something out.'

Sabeena looked at Vikram and then turned her eyes to Neha and Madhu, her eyes conveying deep gratitude.

***

Sudarshan and Balwant spent three days in New Delhi organising flight tickets and completing the necessary documentation for Vikram's departure to Oxford. The family was excited, but also a little nervous. No one they knew had travelled to the United Kingdom from the Quarters.

A young man had won a scholarship to the Patrice Lumumba Friendship University in Moscow, a few years ago—that was the only time anyone from the

Quarters had gone overseas.

Many people did not even want to go that far. A few even considered travelling across the seven seas a kind of punishment.

'Your child should stay in front of your eyes. A job in the railways is the best. Why go so far away to the land where they eat beef?' observed *Pundit Ji*.

August, the month of Vikram's departure to Oxford, finally arrived.

Professor William had sent Vikram a long coat made of Scottish wool to protect him from the long, cold British winters. His mother had hand-knitted two sweaters, along with a scarf, gloves, socks and a cap.

Everyone at home—and Madhu—was frantically helping Vikram pack everything he might need in Oxford. Neha and Madhu had cooked a hundred parathas and several other snacks that could, they thought, last him a month. Vikram had also bought a small pressure cooker.

Over fifty neighbours, relatives and friends turned up at the Tundla railway station to see Vikram off at Platform 1. There was excitement, but also a tinge of sadness and anxiety. His mother was mostly in tears. Neha and Madhu's eyes had turned red from crying off and on, all morning.

His father and Balwant would accompany him right up to the Air India flight from Delhi's Palam

Airport the following night. Soon the Calcutta-Delhi Kalka Mail, powered by Vikram's favourite WP steam locomotive, arrived, instantly transforming the platform into a folk fair, complete with its signature sounds, smells and chaos.

'*Chai-chai-chai, cutlets-cutlets, chole-chole—spicy chole, dalmoth-dalmoth-dalmoth, Agra-ka-pethaaaa!*' cried vendors and hawkers, overwhelming the atmosphere. Coolies in their red shirts pushed anyone who got in their way.

Vikram touched his mother's feet in farewell, just as the train guard blew his whistle signalling all passengers to board the train immediately. The train was about to move when Neha spotted Sabeena in the forest of people on the platform. She grabbed her by her arm and dragged her to the window where Vikram was seated. He immediately jumped out of the coach and hugged her, leaving her visibly pleased and happy.

She handed him a small gift, which he quickly unwrapped—*'My Experiments with Truth'*, the autobiography of Mahatma Gandhi. He was deeply moved and hugged her again before climbing back into the train.

Palam Airport was chaotic, with hundreds crowding every corner to see off their loved ones. Vikram bade goodbye to his father and Balwant Uncle as they helped him load all his baggage into a trolley for the departure gate.

'Stay away from English girls. They're fine as girlfriends, but not as wives,' Balwant Uncle advised teasingly, giving him a big hug. 'I'm only joking—don't take it seriously. Girls are girls, women are women—the world over. Study hard and enjoy your life there.'

Vikram soon boarded the aircraft—a new Air India Boeing 747, popularly known as the Jumbo Jet. He had a window seat. It was his first time ever on a flight, and he was excited.

The captain announced that the journey to London Heathrow would take fourteen hours, with a stopover in Beirut for refuelling. Take-off was an exhilarating and unforgettable experience. Once the plane reached cruising altitude, the cabin lights were turned on.

Three hours into the flight, small screens dropped from the ceiling, all across the cabin to play a Bollywood blockbuster. Vikram was now starting to feel tired. He tried watching the movie, but his mind kept drifting back to Tundla—to his father, mother, sister, and Madhu. And to Sabeena—more than anyone else.

Her sad, disturbed, and withdrawn face at the railways station would not leave his mind. He looked around in an effort to distract himself, but all he could see was Sabeena. Her face appeared everywhere—on the movie screen, on the windows, on the ceiling, on the curtains.

Vikram had never experienced anything like that before.

Am I missing her? But why? he asked himself. Maybe I am just worried about her welfare… 'he answered himself.

He got up and retrieved the book she had gifted him from his handbag from the overhead storage bin. He kissed it, treating it like something precious, surprising himself.

He tried to sleep, but sleep eluded him. He looked out of the window. A vast and open sky stretched before him—but even that view was interrupted by Sabeena's face. The sky was Sabeena. The ocean below was Sabeena. The cabin inside was Sabeena.

Suddenly, everything he saw was—Sabeena.

Vikram could not rest even for a moment. He told himself it was probably his concern for her which was manifesting in this way.

He concluded that emotions for the people one cares about can grow more intense when one is far away from them. It couldn't be anything else.

12

Vikram fell in love with Oxford even before he had checked into Castle House, the students' accommodation. Ancient buildings, majestic lamp posts, sprawling trees, everything caught his eye as his bus drove into the university town from Heathrow. The sky was overcast, with a thin sheet of rain keeping the world grey, a lovely welcome for a young man from a distant little town in India, used to 42-degree summers and endless dust. The far cooler Oxford felt like heaven in comparison.

His room was quite basic, but it had everything he needed for his stay. Vikram said hello to the girl next door, Caroline who had arrived from Canada. They would be classmates and would share a kitchen. Vikram hurriedly dumped his stuff in his room and rushed for a city tour on foot, with the help of a map he was handed at check-in. He wanted to familiarise himself with the place at the earliest.

Carrying an umbrella did not come naturally to Vikram. He forgot to carry one in his rush to hit the road. He had to return to his room to collect it. The air smelled fresh; the drizzle felt soft and sweet. He felt no jet lag or tiredness, even after the long journey from India. His mind wandered back and forth between Oxford—Madhu, Neha and Sabeena; he hoped they could also be with him here some day.

His first stop was at an iconic bookshop on the road behind the Randolph Hotel, which he was told was the favourite of many visiting the university. He had never seen a bookshop with such a vast collection, and so filled with book lovers—every inch of the three floors was taken over by them, flipping through the books ever so gently and respectfully. Vikram spent an hour there. He did not have any spare money to buy a book, but knew he would have access to libraries very soon. Vikram spent the next day hopping across different book shops in Oxford. He also passed by St John's College, a magnificent building, and remembered his college back in Agra, fondly.

The first few days were memorable. Very soon, he began to feel at home. He sat down to write two letters: one to Madhu and the other to Neha, sharing all he had experienced so far, and how much he missed them. The letter to Madhu was a little longer, with many sub-paragraphs addressed to Sabeena. Vikram wanted Madhu to make sure Sabeena was safe.

The Oxford Institute of New Economics and Finance had a great campus, quaint yet modern in terms of required infrastructure and facilities. Faculty and students hailed from as many as forty-seven countries, including Bhutan, Pakistan, and China. The majority, however, belonged to either side of the Atlantic. North Americans and the Europeans dominated the campus and campus life.

The South Asian community was small, but close-knit, hanging out together, often even cooking *rajma-chawal* and *matar paneer* together. The groups of students from Africa were the most active; they even had their own band and football team.

Vikram melted into campus life like butter in hot *pulao*. He joined three different societies and the prestigious Future Investment Bankers' Club. The classrooms were well equipped. The faculty was not only highly accomplished but friendly, open, and warm towards the students. The Institute was like a new universe for Vikram. Known for its long and rich traditions, customs and values, it bore similarities to St John's, which still followed many old British traditions, which helped Vikram transition to Oxford without too many challenges. However, he soon realised that the Institute was designed for white Europeans and North Americans.

Vikram noticed an announcement for electing the new Student Council for the academic year and decided to run for it. No Asian had been elected to the prestigious post, but he decided to give it a shot and promised to give it his all. The contest turned out to be much tougher than he had thought. His opponent was James Hampton, the only son of a celebrated professor of economics at Harvard. He was a graduate from an Ivy League university and a gifted orator. Vikram's strategy was not to confront him in any area where he had an edge. In fact, he generously complimented him on all his strengths, which were thanks to his privileged background.

Vikram focused on personal contact with every voter, communicating who he was, where he had come from, his story, his humility, his values.

His narrative was: *'I have seen all shades of life, and shall use all my experience for the benefit of every member of the student community.'*

He went into everything with humility. The students loved it. James was a great candidate, but Vikram felt more like one of them. Vikram also did exceptionally well in two campaign debates: *'Is Capitalism Dead?'* and *'Why Asia, Africa and Latin America Love Democratic Socialism.'*

Frustrated, James called Vikram, 'an alien to Western norms, beliefs and civilisation and, hence, unfit and unacceptable for the post.' Vikram refused to engage or respond, and laughed it off saying, 'I am new but not alien.'

Vikram won the election. His friend, Liv Garland,

from Edinburgh, was elected Secretary. There were celebrations at Vikram's home back in India. Sabeena sent a sweet congratulatory card.

Vikram shifted his focus entirely to his studies and Council work. He promised himself a distinction in his degree. He also remained acutely aware of the responsibility he carried, being the first elected Indian Council President at such an iconic institution. He reworked his daily calendar in an effort to use his time prudently. His letters to loved ones back home also reduced in frequency to just once a month.

He was an active participant in the Future Investment Bankers' Club, popularly known as the Money Dreamers Group or MDG. They met every Friday after dinner to discuss trends and ideas in investment banking and related fields like hedge funds. Vikram loved the creative energy and talks at the MDG meetings. To his surprise, he discovered his own keen interest in investment banking—and especially in hedge funds—and soon emerged as the most enthusiastic participant in these meetings.

MDG often invited senior investment bankers and hedge fund managers from London to speak over informal drinks, followed by Q-and-A sessions.

Vikram followed a rigorous daily routine, prioritising his time between the library, class lectures, Council work and MDG meetings. He made it a point to attend all guest lectures—often delivered by top CEOs, ministers, economists, thinkers and celebrities. He would go to bed at 2 am and be up by 6.30 am. He was truly on a mission.

The Council met every Thursday evening in its office within the main administrative building. The first five meetings had been very productive with some landmark decisions such as setting up a stress management clinic, launching a support centre for students from Asia, Africa and Latin America, and publishing *'The International Pages'*, a weekly newspaper for the students.

The sixth Council meeting went on till midnight, with heated debates over how to respond to the administration's decision to raise the students' accommodation fees from January. The Council was divided: some favoured negotiations with the Dean, others called for a strike.

Vikram argued against the protest.

'We are students from across the world here. Many of us are here because of great sacrifices back home, so that we can study and build a good future for ourselves. Let's try negotiations, first.'

Another Council member, Eva Hansen, and a few others, supported him strongly. Though, several continued to demand tough action, remaining in favour of the protest. Finally, fortunately, the house decided to go along with Vikram, with the caveat that if negotiations failed within a week, the Council would call a protest on the campus. A communication was prepared and sent to the Institute's Dean within the hour.

The episode had, however, exposed Vikram to the reality of racism. Many Western students had opposed him without clear reason. Some refused to engage with him at all. Vikram chose to take it all in his stride, concluding that things would settle in time.

That night, Vikram had just settled down at his desk, back in his room, when he heard a soft knock on his door. At first, he ignored it, thinking it came from the upper floor. But the knock came again, persistent. He got up and opened the door.

Eva Hansen stood there.

They had never spoken outside Council meetings.

'Hi Eva, what's the matter?' Vikram asked.

She stood silently for a moment, then said, 'Do I look ugly to you?'

'What?' asked Vikram, surprised by the question. 'Did I hurt you in the meeting today? Or did I say something you did not like?'

'I have been watching you for the past few meetings, but you refused to engage. Why? Do I look that bad?'

'I just didn't notice, Vikram replied honestly. I'm still not very comfortable around girls, except those I've grown up with.

'But you are a brilliant girl, and very articulate. I noticed that in the very first Council meeting. You are exceptional.'

'Let's go for a midnight walk under the stars. It's beautiful tonight,' she said suddenly, practically forcing him to accompany her.

Before he realised it, they were out under the sky, with Eva holding a reluctant Vikram's hand.

Eva was born in Boston to a Swedish father and a French mother. She was tall, blonde and strikingly beautiful, with sharp features and long, flowing hair.

'You have wonderful hair and the most attractive nose I've ever seen,' Vikram told her.

'Nose?' she laughed. 'No one's ever complimented my nose before! Is that how you talk to your girlfriend back home?'

'I don't have a girlfriend back home. I don't have time for a girlfriend.'

'No time for a girlfriend?' Eva asked, surprised. 'You mean you have never been in love?'

'Never.' Vikram replied. 'Why? Are you surprised?'

'Yes, I am. You're a good-looking guy. I would've imagined you have been in love multiple times by now.'

'Eastern cultures are different from the West. Education, security, jobs, and family come before love in our societies. You'd need to live there to understand what I mean.'

'This sounds depressing,' Eva remarked.

'We are different—that's all. I wouldn't call it depressing. Every society, every country is different. My priority is to secure my life first.'

'I think you have a fair point,' Eva conceded.

They walked miles that night, sharing their family stories. Eva was moved to tears by Vikram's family saga—and particularly by his yearning for a home—after his family lost everything in the Partition. Eventually, they entered a sprawling cemetery. Eva settled on a bench nestled between three old graves.

The place felt more like an ashram or monastery than a graveyard—peaceful and timeless.

'I like this place,' Vikram said. Eva gently held his arm. They sat there until they heard the birds chirping.

'I liked you the moment I saw you in the Council meeting, Eva said. 'You have an innocent face.'

'I'm surprised how quickly we've got to know each other—about our families, everything. It feels like some natural force is pushing us towards each other. I feel like I have known you for ages. I have never experienced anything like this before,' said Vikram.

Vikram and Eva were soon a couple—always seen together in libraries, cafes, bookshops, meetings, parks and on the streets. They often cooked dinner together. Eva introduced him to Swedish and French recipes, and quickly developed a taste for Indian *matar paneer* and mushroom masala curry.

Vikram wrote a long letter to Madhu and Neha, sharing details about his deep friendship with Eva. He called her 'a divinely gorgeous and intelligent girl,' and enclosed a few photographs of Eva.

'I don't know if I love her but I love her company. I like everything about her—what she does, wears, says, likes, reads. If this is love, then I think I am in love, and for the first time in my life,' he wrote.

Neha and the Sarhadi family received the news with some caution, writing back that he should focus on his studies first.

Sabeena was never far from Vikram's mind. When her father passed away, he sent her a letter of condolence, reminding her that she was not alone—they were all with her. He also advised her not to lose focus on her Master's degree in Economics.

Sabeena wrote back thanking him and asking him to take care. 'Madhu told me about your girlfriend. I'm sure she's beautiful and smart like you. Please convey my love to her. I wish you both a great future, together.'

Oxford had transformed Vikram. That shy and insecure boy from Tundla was history. He had become a confident young man, a quick learner, and proud of his Eastern roots and upbringing. Yet, he had learned to feel at ease in any Western setting too. For him, it wasn't East versus West—he believed in embracing the best of both worlds. The inflammatory, anti-migrant rhetoric and politics in Britain, however, outraged him, leaving him feeling unwelcome. But he would passionately argue that it would never go mainstream, thanks to the Isles' historical linkages and interdependence with the Commonwealth countries across the world.

But his yearning for a home continued to dog him. He was clear he would return to India, eventually. He longed to visit home during breaks to meet his family and friends, or to invite them over to Oxford, but neither he nor they could afford it financially.

The Institute soon broke for the Christmas holiday. It was winter, getting colder and colder, but Vikram and Eva continued their midnight walks, ending up at the graveyard bench. They decided to holiday in Scotland for two weeks, travelling by train.

'That's going to be great fun. I have never been there before,' said Eva, and then drew Vikram into an embrace. She kissed him. Their bodies melted into each other. Every night, they returned to the same bench before they left for Edinburgh. Their love deepened. They began dreaming of a shared future together.

Eva told Vikram that her parents would also be there in Edinburgh for two days and that they would all be staying in the same hotel as her father's guests.

'They are desperate to meet you.'

'Wonderful, I look forward to seeing them,' Vikram replied.

They took a train to Scotland, stopped over at Leuchars and spent a couple of days in St Andrews, a postcard-perfect town, famed for being the birthplace of golf and for the University of St Andrews, one of the greatest educational institutions in the world. Everything here was scenic, historical and worth visiting. Eva and Vikram had never seen a university more beautiful than St Andrews.

On the train to Edinburgh, Vikram said, '*A speeding train in picturesque Scotland, a window seat and your companionship, and your hand in my hand...I could not have asked for more, I could not have wished for more.*'

Eva's parents were waiting in the hotel lobby.

'Happy to meet you, *Vikraaamm!*' said Eva's father, shaking Vikram's hand. 'Eva tells me you're from India. How interesting. I have never been to India...too many poor people.'

'We still have economic poverty in parts of India, but culturally, spiritually and socially we are a prosperous country, sir,' Vikram responded calmly. 'We will overcome economic poverty in the coming decades. Colonisation destroyed our basic industries, and it takes generations to rebuild.'

Eva's mother quickly changed the subject to travelling

in Scotland, saying she was very familiar with Edinburgh and its tourists places. She drew up an itinerary for them, strongly recommending them to follow it to get the best out of their stay at minimum cost. Eva and Vikram thanked them for lunch and set off to explore the city.

Eva apologised to Vikram for her father's remarks on poverty in India.

'Let's move on,' Vikram murmured, and kissed her. They spent most of their time in Edinburgh in bookshops, museums, quaint streets and cafes, holding hands, embracing, and eating food from the same plate.

Later, they travelled to Loch Ness in the Scottish Highlands, jokingly hoping to see the Loch Ness Monster. 'I really thought we'd see Nessie,' Eva laughed.

'Don't lose heart. Here's the monster you are looking for.' Vikram twisted his face into a maniacal expression. 'I love this monster,' said Eva, pulling Vikram close for a kiss.

They spent the rest of their holiday walking in the woods, lazing around and reading books under the trees. 'I only need things from this life—to see you everyday and to live among nature,' Vikram told Eva. They returned to the Castle House happier and closer than ever before.

***

The couple volunteered to organise the next MDG event, and succeeded in inviting Sir Jon Dunes, a celebrated billionaire investment banker, as the guest speaker. They had travelled to London twice to persuade him to accept the invite.

Vikram introduced the honoured guest and moderated the session. The event was an unprecedented success, with the room overflowing with participants.

Sir Dunes invited Vikram and Eva to his office in London. Sharp as an eagle, he sensed their talent and potential, and had done his due diligence on the duo.

Lunch with Sir Dunes, two weeks later, in London turned out to be a life changer. His large office in the heart of the financial district, housed over two hundred executives and radiated power, success, class and sophistication. Sir Dunes invited Vikram and Eva to join him in the launch of a new boutique investment bank, to be based in London and New York. 'I will hold fifty per cent and you two will each hold, twenty-five per cent. I will put in the initial investment.'

'But we have no experience,' Eva pointed out, looking at Vikram in amazement.

'You will undergo six months of on-the-job training in my company, starting, right after your final examinations,' Sir Dunes replied.

'I'm in the business of investment—not just in markets, but in people and relationships. I see talent in both of you.'

Vikram and Eva were stunned and did not know how to react. They celebrated the news, though they couldn't quite grasp why Sir Dunes was being so generous.

Even as things in his personal and professional life seemed to be falling into place, Vikram began to experience something strange. The more he loved Eva, the more he thought of Sabeena.

Eva was his present love—his life, his future. But at the same time Sabeena began to occupy more and more space of his inner world and mind. He could not understand it, and it worried him.

Sometimes, he wondered if his feelings for Sabeena were tangled up with his longing for home. Perhaps, she had become a symbol of all he had left behind—the unresolved struggle with his roots, his unfinished past.

But his life was moving forward and changing at such a fast pace that it was difficult for him to reconcile his feelings; he had no option but to shelve his thoughts—for now.

Time flew.

After their final examinations, Vikram and Eva rented a small studio apartment in London and began their on-the-job training. Dreams of success and money danced before them.

They were on the cusp of an amazing and wonderful life.

Or so they thought.

13

The flight to Stockholm was turbulent. But the occasion for travel was joyful—Vikram and Eva had passed their exams with distinctions.

Eva introduced Vikram to her cousins. One of them, an investment banker, took them around the city, starting with the famous Gamla Stan, known for its cobbled streets, gourmet restaurants and exclusive stores. They spent the first night in a rented cabin in Grinda. Vikram loved the place so much that he promised Eva to return to the same cabin in the archipelago for their honeymoon after their marriage.

'I thought you would take me to Venice or Prague,' Eva teased him.

They flew north to Lapland in the Swedish Arctic, then travelled by road to Narvik, a beautiful Norwegian town. Vikram fell in love with Arctic Scandinavia—its rugged and pristine nature moved him deeply.

Back from their holidays, Eva and Vikram quickly got down to business: Dune, Sarhadi, Hansen and Partners—or DSH Partners. Vikram performed a brief *Ganesh Puja* at the new office, following the Hindu tradition of invoking blessings before launching a new project, mission or anything new.

The business was launched with a lavish party at a luxury hotel in Mayfair. The evening was a glitzy affair. Four senior British cabinet ministers attended, along with the who's who of the London business world. The American Ambassador and the Indian High Commissioner also made appearances. Eva and Vikram were thrilled and made the most of the evening, initiating relationships with most of the assembled movers and shakers.

'A good relationship is like a blank cheque. Always handle it with utmost care and sensitivity,' Sir Dunes whispered in their ears, as he introduced the duo to some of the most influential guests.

The couple soon moved into a two-bedroom apartment, over the next weekend, courtesy of DSH Partners. The new apartment was a luxury—elegant and modern and closer to the office. They entered the business determined to meet every weekly, monthly and quarterly milestone.

'Make deals with a killer's instinct. Offense, not defence,' Sir Dunes counselled them in those early days.

They made a pact to always be home by 9 pm when in London, and to reserve the weekends for each other. Living together, they designed their routine to minimise interfering in each other's personal beliefs and faith. Vikram often woke up early to pray briefly. They were, in many ways, very different, but they looked wonderful together—made for each other. What united them was their shared ambition—to make DSH a huge success and to build a life that was both meaningful and joyful.

Their routine was abruptly disrupted one day when Sabeena sent Vikram a letter—the first since his arrival in England. Her letter was filled with anguish. She wrote about intense loneliness, and how every morning brought a new layer of darkness into her gloomy life. She described in harrowing details about how two male members of her husband's extended family had unsuccessfully tried to rape her, while her husband was admitted to a hospital in Firozabad for tuberculosis.

Only in the last paragraph, she shared more devastating news:

> *My husband died of pancreatic tuberculosis. He was buried earlier this month. I am now alone—all alone in this world. I miss my father. And I miss you a lot. Please help me stay alive and sane.*
>
> *I love you —Sabeena.*

Vikram was shocked. He immediately wrote back offering his deepest sympathies, advising her to move out of her husband's house. He encouraged her to look for a teaching job or give private tuitions in economics to keep herself busy and earn an income. He also offered to send her some money.

He sent the reply via Madhu, requesting her to look after Sabeena. Vikram also reached out to the head of a school in Tundla, requesting that Sabeena be considered for a teaching position.

14

Sudarshan Sarhadi had just handed over charge of the Howrah-Amritsar Express locomotive to the new driver. It was pitch dark as he left the station at midnight, walking through the Company Garden. He wore a thick wooden cap and a Chester overcoat, provided by the railways, as part of his winter uniform.

As he crossed the vast grounds, he realised he was being followed. Glancing over his shoulder, he saw a tall man with his face covered with a black monkey cap. Sudarshan quickened his pace. But the man, realising he had been spotted, sprinted ahead and attacked him with a knife.

Thinking he was being robbed, Sudarshan offered to hand over his wallet, gold ring and wristwatch. But the attacker shoved him off his feet without a word, and tried to pin him down to the ground. He was tall, strong and well built. But Sudarshan, sensing that this was no robbery but an attempt to kill him, fought back fiercely, shouting and kicking. He managed to get the attacker off his body, but the man pierced his abdomen with his knife. He tried to slash Sudarshan's throat or neck, but did not succeed, as Sudarshan, filled with adrenaline, landed several forceful blows and punches on his face.

Realising he had failed, the attacker fled into the darkness before his identity could be revealed. Sudarshan limped home, bleeding and in shock. Lakshmi and Neha burst into frenzied wails on seeing his bloodied clothes and called Balwant. Together, they rushed him to the hospital.

'He has suffered two knife wounds, but they have missed his vital organs,' the attending doctor reported. 'He will need stitches and bedrest until the wound heals. We need to inform the police.'

Neha made an ISD call, informing Vikram about the attack. She wept and asked her brother to come home.

Vikram arrived in India on the first available flight. The whole family was in shock.

The police began investigating the attack.

'This is clearly a case of attempted murder,' the investigating officer concluded.

'To kill him? But why?' cried Lakshmi.

'Think if someone holds a grudge against your family, or against your husband. In most cases, there's either some rivalry or family dispute,' the officer reasoned.

'My father is on good terms with everyone. I can't imagine anyone wanting to harm him,' Vikram said, bewildered.

Neha practically lived at the hospital, taking care of her father. Sabeena assisted Neha. Lakshmi and Vikram stayed the nights, so the two girls could go home and rest. Madhu arrived daily to help with Vikram. Balwant dropped in as often as he could. Vikram and Sabeena could only briefly enquire about each other—but hardly had the opportunity to speak further.

When the doctors reassured Vikram that his father would soon be discharged, he decided to fly back to London. However, the incident deeply troubled him, and he felt terrified at the prospect of losing his father.

The police investigation eventually led to the discovery of the sudden emergence of a dry-fruit seller in the town two weeks ago, and his equally sudden disappearance. They made enquiries in nearby towns, but no one knew anything more about the man, except that he was quite tall, and didn't seem interested in hawking his wares. In the end, several weeks of investigation led to very little progress, so they had to close the matter in the absence of any evidence. The Sarhadis pleaded with the police not to drop the investigation, but to no avail.

With Vikram leaving, Lakshmi took to prayers and intense meditation. She began visiting the temple three times a day. Neha acquired a constant look of fear, and became cautious about leaving the house. Madhu, and Sabeena, who had moved back to the Basti, became pillars of support for the family.

15

Vikram returned to London, hoping to leave the chaos of Tundla behind. The trip back home in those difficult circumstances had brought him grief and anxiety, but back in the UK, he quickly settled into his old routine with Eva. The couple spent long hours in the office, closing deals with clients in the United States and beyond. Working lunches at posh restaurants, meetings with financial powerhouses, and visits to Amsterdam, Paris, Frankfurt and other business hotspots became part of their daily life. DSH Partners delivered encouraging results in their first two quarters. Sir Dunes hosted a celebratory lunch at the office to celebrate the achievement and congratulated the pair, wishing them success for the firm's New York expansion.

They had hired four executives for their American office, including James Mathew, a close friend of Eva's from Oxford. Eva and Vikram appointed Mathew as the head of their New York office and their operations in the United States, Canada and Mexico. They were building a formidable team.

Vikram liked New York, but soon realised it wasn't his kind of city.

'This is a great city to work in; to make money and grow professionally but I don't like the way it overwhelms me. It tells me to live the way it wants,' he remarked.

Eva laughed, 'That's harsh, darling. This city has so much vivacity that even the dead in New York would get up and start working and dancing once again.'

Vikram responded, 'Precisely, that's what I meant. The city decides everything for you.'

They flew to Boston for the weekend to visit Eva's parents and tour the city's great universities, Harvard and MIT. Vikram quickly sensed that Eva's father was not too happy with his daughter's choice of an Indian boyfriend. He was shocked when he overheard the man describing him as a 'dark, unimpressive character' in a conversation with his wife, after Eva and Vikram had left the dining room to watch the news in the lounge.

Eva's father never addressed Vikram with respect. He was rude and dismissive, especially since he realised that Eva was serious about Vikram. One evening, he came up from behind Vikram as he was browsing a bookshelf in the living room. All the books were about the West, and the greatness of its history.

'The United States is one of the few nations in the world that has produced real heroes,' Eva's father announced, palming a book about Jefferson.

'I'll send you a few books on India and Mahatma Gandhi—' Vikram began enthusiastically.

'Thanks, but I am not interested in the Gandhi and Mandela types,' Eva's father said, cutting Vikram short. 'Is your family in business back home?'

'No, my father is a loco-driver in the railways and my mother takes care of the house,' said Vikram, honestly.

'I pity you,' the older man replied. 'Eva mentioned you love the railways. You should go back and join the railways as well. You're built for it.'

Vikram was taken aback, and snapped. 'I will do what I want to do. I'm already doing what I like. I don't need your advice.'

The Boston trip rapidly became unpleasant for Vikram. He resolved never to return to Boston or interact with Eva's rude and racist father. After launching the New York office, Eva and Vikram returned to London, but Vikram felt his dignity had been deeply wounded.

'Such a terrible man cannot be the father of a woman as wonderful as my Eva,' he wrote in a message to Madhu.

He took a week off and flew unannounced to Tundla, much to everyone's surprise and joy. Balwant invited him over to his house for a special meal, as did several neighbours. He stopped for a prayer at the

Hanuman Temple and chatted with *Pundit Ji.* Local journalists came seeking interviews with him, but he declined saying he had nothing to say. In small towns like Tundla, going abroad was a big deal. Vikram had landed in the world of investment banking, and that too in the West. Vikram's name had been in the local media with stories about his success for some time now.

He managed to meet and speak with Sabeena, one evening and they went on a long walk.

'When do you plan to marry Eva?' Sabeena asked, in a sad and broken voice.

'I have not thought about it seriously yet,' Vikram replied.

'She must be very beautiful?'

'She is. She's wonderful and I love her. She's my first love.'

'Eva is a lucky girl.'

'I know for sure that I'm lucky. She's beautiful, elegant, and brilliant. A rare combination,' he said then added, with a smile, 'Just like you.'

'Do not compare me to her. I'm a most unfortunate person. How can you compare us?' Sabeena muttered. 'My father is gone. My husband is gone. I'm alone in the world. But it's also liberating. I have no worries, no anxieties. I think only of myself now,' she said. 'I'm in a different world.'

'Focus on yourself. You are a university topper in MA

Economics. You will find a good job soon. Move out of the Basti to some better place where you can find a job.'

'No, I won't move out of the Basti. I have now become part of the support system there. Children depend on me for help with their homework. Women rely on me for their small but critical needs, like opening a bank account or handling their cash. Or running their small businesses like laundry or making *papad*. They are like my extended family now. I feel safe there.'

'I understand, but remember I am here, if you need anything—money, books, whatever.'

'You caring for me is more than enough, I don't want to be greedy and lose you. I'll always love you. You don't have to return my love.'

Sabeena handed Vikram a dried night jasmine flower, a token of her feelings. 'Unfortunately, it's not the season of the night jasmine, or I would have given you a fresh flower.'

'Thank you. That's so thoughtful,' said Vikram, as held her hand and pressed it affectionately.

The night had begun to get dark. The sky looked like a platter with millions of lamps arranged across it carelessly.

Sabeena pointed towards the North Star and said, 'Vikram, I often spend my nights staring and speaking with this star. I know England lies to the north. This star connects me to you.'

Vikram moved by her words and the depth of her love, said, 'You're the most beautiful soul in the world.'

Sabeena smiled, but her sad eyes betrayed sorrow and the many unanswered questions she still held back.

***

Neha wanted to know her brother's marriage plans, but he said he did not have much to share on the matter at this stage. Neha did not disapprove of Eva, but she repeatedly cautioned him against marrying a Western girl.

She said, 'It's okay to have a European girlfriend, but for marriage, only an Indian girl will make you happy.'

Her words irritated Vikram, forcing him to snap back at times, 'I came here for a break, to meet you all, not to discuss marriage.'

Balwant, who had dropped in one evening, sided with Vikram, 'Let him enjoy his life with Eva. Let them know and discover each other first.'

Vikram shared his irritation with Madhu as well.

'Ignore them and do what you want,' was her simple advice. 'I'm glad you are in love. It's about time.'

'Yes. It's such a wonderful feeling. Everything looks better, more beautiful now,' said Vikram.

Madhu sighed. 'My parents want to marry me to a boy from our caste that they have chosen. He also works in the railways. But I don't want to get married yet. I want to move to New Delhi and pursue a PhD, from a reputed place like DU or JNU. I want to be a professor, an accomplished professor.'

'You must fulfil your dream.'

'It's not that easy for girls.'

'...but marrying someone you don't want will be worse. We've seen what Sabeena went through. And I'm here for you; I have resources too. I can help you in any way you want.'

'Let me think things through.'

The conversation drifted away to other things. Vikram admitted his yearning for a home had only grown since his new life in England. He loved Tundla and had, somewhere deep within, prepared himself to call it his home, anchor and future.

'Ramkund will be in my heart, but I can never feel close to it the way I feel rooted in Tundla.'

Madhu hugged him. Both had tears in their eyes. They had a deep and special bond. Vikram saw Madhu as his pillar of strength. And for Madhu, he was the rock she could count upon anytime.

The trip passed quickly. Back in London, Eva greeted Vikram at the airport with a hug and a kiss 'I can't live without you, not even for a day. Promise me you will never leave me alone, ever again.'

Eva then told him about her discussions with Sir

Dunes about focusing more on New York, Texas, and California, for expanding their business. They planned to rent an apartment in New York City and spend two weeks there each month. Vikram said he was happy to do anything that would help them grow the firm.

DSH Partners trebled in size the following year. Eva and Vikram were among the ten most talked about young investment and hedge fund bankers in Western Europe and New York. Sir Dunes threw a glitzy party in New York to celebrate their achievements. The financial media was full of stories about the two new young millionaires. Eva and Vikram bought a Jaguar. Vikram gifted a brand-new Fiat to his family back home—the first ever car in Tundla. Celebrations followed both in London and Tundla.

But success came at a cost. Life for Eva and Vikram grew busier, leaving them with less and less time for each other. Their original commitment to always spend weekends together was sacrificed to their success. Often, they crossed each other mid-air over the Atlantic—Eva returning from New York and Vikram on his way to New York. Nights were increasingly spent in hotels, in Munich, Amsterdam, Frankfurt, Houston, Los Angeles and Brussels. They had apartments in New York and London. Eva wanted a small holiday apartment in Cannes. Vikram loved the idea and went along with it. They were proud of their achievements and all that they now owned but craved their quiet weekends again.

Eva proposed a short holiday in Cannes, and they spent a lazy week enjoying the sun and food.

'I want to retire in Cannes when we turn forty,' Vikram said. 'I will read and write and maybe grow grapes and make wine.'

'I can't wait for the future.'

16

DSH Partners had come a long way. Sir Dunes, known for his stinginess in offering compliments, commended Vikram and Eva, calling them '*gems in my group*'. Strong indications suggested he had begun to see Vikram as his probable successor.

Vikram was surprised at his own success. His move to diversify into the hedge fund business, with a focus on the United States, had contributed handsomely to the DSH bottom-line. But it had all come at a cost. Frequent trips across the world had burnt him out emotionally and mentally. The time he spent with Eva had shrunk to a trickle, leaving them both irritated, edgy and unfulfilled. They could feel themselves drifting apart.

Eva began insisting on locking their relationship into a marriage and moving to New York, lock, stock and barrel.

'Of what value is money, if we don't have time for each other?' she would ask him, almost ritually, over the phone. 'We are both on the wrong side of our twenties. We have everything we need and yet we aren't happy. We are barely together.'

Eventually, they decided to take a weekend off to go to Venice to clear their heads and figure their way forward.

Venice, the city of love, put Eva in a good mood as soon as she touched down at Marco Polo airport. The couple took a long gondola ride and walking tour, exploring cafes, shops and tiny lanes. In a fit of love, Vikram lifted Eva by the waist and twirled her around, indulging in a long deep kiss.

They bought Murano glass artifacts and chandeliers for their apartment. Eva spoke excitedly about designing their New York apartment. Vikram looked at her sideways and kept his silence.

At dinner, Vikram, looked a bit stressed and preoccupied.

Eva, still caught up in her own world, pulled out a sheet of paper with some notes, and said, 'Honey, let's get married next month in Boston, and relocate to New York. Mathew said he will take care of all the necessary arrangements. We just have to get there.'

Stunned, Vikram spent several minutes recovering his composure before speaking. 'I'm too stressed to think of marriage, Eva. We love each other so much and that's all that matters. And relocating to New York? Losing London? This is too much change, and in too little time.'

Other things were on his mind too. Of late, he had been missing his family back home miserably.

'I miss my family. I miss Tundla. Moving to New York permanently would mean being even farther away from them.'

'But you have so much going for you in New York, Vikram. Your job, me. You'll be a billionaire before you know it.'

'What if we get married in New Delhi and move there instead? We could continue to run our firm from India, with a monthly trip to London,' Vikram proposed pensively.

'You want me to move to India, to live there?' Eva's eyes widened like saucers. 'Are you crazy? Don't you know how unsafe your country is for women?' Vikram tried to calm her, but she went on. 'My dad says your country is also among the dirtiest in the world,' she said tersely, ignoring his counter-arguments.

'Your dad?' Vikram's voice was icy. 'So, he's the one behind your plan.'

'Yes, he is. Why not? He's my father.'

'Your father's a racist man, Eva. You know what he said to me when we visited him in Boston?' Vikram's voice was now icier.

Eva realised she had gone too far. The conversation ended without any conclusion. The couple felt isolated—each consumed by their own intense wants and feelings.

It was the worst evening they had ever spent together.

They ordered a water taxi and returned to their hotel suite. They did not exchange a word until the next morning when they decided to cut the trip short and return to London on the first available flight.

Vikram was firm that he would not move to New York.

When Eva made another attempt to convince him to move, he told her, 'I love you deeply and I want to spend the rest of my life with you. But I cannot move to the United States. I don't want to be even further away from my home and roots. If I cannot access my ancestral home, at least I want to remain close to the adopted home where I was born.'

Eva, exaperated by his reluctance, now gave him an ultimatum.

'Enough is enough, Vikram. I need to move back to New York. You can come with me, or I'll go myself.'

Vikram was devastated. He knew her well. He knew it was all over.

He took a long walk through Hyde Park, returning to their apartment after three hours—barely able to walk—only to find Eva packed and ready to leave their home. She checked into a hotel that evening.

The next morning, she sent in her resignation to DSH Partners, and put her shares in the firm up for sale.

Their shared dream had gone up in flames.

Appalled and depressed, Vikram soon followed suit. He resigned from the company, vacated the apartment and checked into a hotel. Sir Dunes made every effort to convince them to stay, but it was of no use.

Sir Dunes forced the two of them to meet him over lunch.

'You shouldn't let your personal differences destroy your future,' he told them sternly. 'You are both stars in the investment and hedge fund industry.'

'Stars are made of different material. You cannot behave like ordinary people. You are still in your late twenties, your life and careers have just started, and you're throwing it all away over one disagreement. Just imagine the future awaiting you. Don't behave like teenagers.'

But Eva and Vikram remained adamant. They could no longer even look at each other.

Sir Dunes realised it was pointless in convincing them any further. But he came under criticism from his peers in London for trusting and patronising this young couple so much.

He announced in a press release that he would be buying out the ex-couple's shares and renaming the firm. Eva and Vikram both made over seven million dollars each selling their shares in the firm. The actual value of their shares was much higher, but their anger and sadness made them want to leave as quickly as possible.

Vikram made up his mind to return to Tundla as soon as possible. He had earned enough money to live comfortably for the rest of his life. Yet, he felt betrayed and terribly lonely in London. But he resisted writing back home to his family or Madhu and Sabeena. He didn't want to explain himself.

He applied for a visa to visit Ramkund on his way home, but after sitting on his visa application for several weeks, the Pakistani embassy in London rejected it. They advised him to reapply for it through the embassy in New Delhi.

Finally, Vikram wrote a letter each to Neha, Madhu and Sabeena, informing them about his break up with Eva. He also announced he would soon be returning to Tundla for good.

His family rejoiced at the news, but they were concerned, for his well-being and career. They had no idea that he had done enough to financially secure not only his, but also their lives. His sister had fallen in love with a former college friend, a Syrian Christian from Kerala. Vikram wrote to her that she would have all his support, and he would pay for the wedding.

In his last weeks in London, Vikram worked hard on a new project he intended to start in Tundla:

Name: *The Ramkund Mission*

Aims: *Help. Support. Advocacy. Awareness. Research. Education. Training.*

Target Groups: *The marginalised, the discriminated, the displaced, the vulnerable, the abandoned.*

Geography: *India and beyond*

Headquarters: *Tundla*

Overseas Office: *London*

On his flight back to India, he kept reading through his plans for the Ramkund Mission, feeling a surge of joy at the prospect of being home again. Although his life felt shattered, this new project appealed so strongly to all his instincts that he couldn't help but look forward to it.

17

Caste is a way of life in India. It is a practice most people are born into, and often, they do not stop to consider how harmful or discriminatory it is. The so-called lower castes were conditioned to blame their fate and bad *karma* of their past birth, for their fate in this life.

Sabeena often wondered about untouchability, and how she was told that she would make anything 'impure' by touching it, and why this shameful practice remained prevalent despite being banned by India's Constitution and laws. Many men, especially upper caste men from the Quarters, lusted after her. But the thought of marrying a Valmiki Dalit, however beautiful, never even crossed their minds. The so-called upper castes discriminated against them without guilt, without any serious urge to change it or reform it. There were few exceptions—mostly idealistic young men and women.

Sabeena hated the very idea of the Basti, a ghetto that

bundled all 'untouchables' separately from society. It was worse than a slum; the practice of a separate settlement for 'untouchables' on the outskirts of a village or in a secluded corner in a city, had existed for centuries, simply because the upper castes did not want to even see them, let alone come into contact, unless they were needed for labour. Living in the Basti, Sabeena felt worse than a captive animal. She was often outraged at the plight of her fellow untouchables, especially the children and women, many of whom had no access to basic needs like milk, nutritious food, or medicines. Renaming them as Valmiki Dalits had not helped. They continued to call them 'untouchables' among themselves.

Sabeena heard about the visit of Professor Dina Nath Shastry, a celebrated scholar on 'anti-untouchability' and the Valmiki Dalit reform movement. She attended the meeting, and approached him, striking up a conversation as soon as his interaction with the community elders ended.

'I find the practice of untouchability soul-destroying,' she approached the professor, himself an 'untouchable', a Valmiki Dalit.

He looked at this young woman, whose words were articulate, whose eyes shone with intelligence, and gave her an encouraging nod. 'Untouchability robs you of soul, your dignity, your confidence. You may get the best education from the best university in the world, but even then, the most illiterate from the upper caste will not accept you. Why has such discrimination and hatred for our fellow human beings been allowed to persist for so many centuries? Calling us Valmiki Dalits has made no difference.

'We untouchables did not matter to rulers, the rich or the high castes. We had to exile ourselves from their spaces. We were allowed in only to clean their latrines and streets or to remove dead animals. We hoped that Independence and the Constitution, whose writing was led by the visionary Babasaheb Ambedkar, would change that. But it hasn't. No real transformation has taken place in our lives. We were, and still are, at the bottom of the social pyramid,' said the professor, his voice choked. 'But we must fight, we must build strength. We have no other option!'

Sabeena felt overwhelmed listening to the professor.

'I am impressed by your reasoning and arguments. You have a great future ahead. Read more, study more,' he advised.

'But why can't the government get rid of this evil?' Sabeena persisted.

'Well, untouchability was declared illegal by the law. It is a punishable offence. But it is still pervasive in society. It is a deep-rooted social problem. Religious and social leaders, and communities need to come forward and join forces. What is needed is the enforcement of laws by the people and society. The government alone cannot do much more. The so-called upper castes are powerful and resourceful. They control everything—political parties, civil services, judiciary, media, industry, banks, educational institutions—all the levers of power. We need to educate ourselves and enter those spaces.'

'I hope and pray that we can rid this country of this disease.'

'You will go a long way. You are exceptionally talented and blessed,' the professor said, showering her with praise. Sabeena thanked him repeatedly.

'This girl is the jewel of your *basti,*' the professor told the community leaders as he rose to leave. The gathered people felt the weight of his words. They congratulated Sabeena with newfound respect.

Sabeena rushed to write a letter to Vikram, eager to share the entire episode. She could not sleep that night.

From then on, people began to assemble at her hut to seek her guidance and advice. She was becoming a leader in the Basti, especially for its women.

The new Sabeena had been born.

18

The Air India flight to New Delhi felt longer than usual. Vikram couldn't sleep a wink. His mind oscillated between his jet-set life in London and the one he was about to build for himself in Tundla.

He hadn't informed his family of his arrival. The Clark Shiraz Hotel at Agra had sent a limousine to pick him up from the airport, where he had booked a room for himself until he had a place at Tundla. The Ramkund Mission was now his life's calling. He had already scheduled a meeting with lawyers, chartered accountants and consultants required to begin the registration of The Ramkund Mission.

'I want this mission to be a world-class organisation, known for excellence and integrity.' He had committed 70 per cent of his savings to the Ramkund Mission and spent considerable time with experts from a Bombay-based architectural firm that would design

'*The Ramkund Mission's*' campus. The firm had surveyed Tundla and the adjoining areas and informed him the funds earmarked for the campus would be enough to build a 30-acre self-sustaining campus, complete with offices and accommodation.

'The campus should look like an *ashram* or a monastery. It should radiate peace and wisdom, serenity and energy, song and joy,' Vikram instructed, his heart firmly set upon his new dream. 'We should plant hundreds and hundreds of trees. Harshringar—the night jasmine—must bloom everywhere. There should be space for dogs, cats, cows, deer, ducks, owls, kingfishers and other creatures to live freely.'

19

Vikram took a train the next day and landed at Tundla, surprising his family and Balwant Uncle. Over rounds of tea and home-cooked snacks, he shared his story, from the breakup with Eva to selling his shares in the investment bank to his Ramkund Mission project. His parents and Neha looked worried at first, wondering if he was okay and had not lost his mental and emotional balance due to the breakup. He reassured them he was alright. Whistles of joy and celebration echoed as Vikram disclosed how much money he had made as a hugely successful investment and hedge fund banker.

'I cannot even write the amount of money in numbers that you said you have already made. Well done my boy,' said Balwant. 'But why do you want to waste your hard-earned money on charity, this Ramkund Mission? Save this money, move to Bombay and start your own investment bank.'

'I think God has helped me earn so much money so quickly so I could live my dreams,' Vikram said, 'I lived a very high-flying life in London and I have concluded that is not what I want. The Ramkund Mission is what I am going to do for the rest of my life.'

'We need to keep all of this secret now. Here people can kill for a very small amount of money. You know how dangerous our area is. Gangs of dacoits and murderers are common here; they are everywhere here. Don't tell anybody of your money or success in London. Say you are building The Mission with the help of contributions from others—some rich people in England.' Lakshmi felt anxious about her son's safety. She was worried about her son, wondering whether the breakup with that American girl had pushed her son towards escapism.

Vikram met Sabeena and Madhu on the side of the football ground and requested them to come over to Agra to meet him at his hotel, which would be his new workplace. He offered to send a car to pick them up and drop them back.

Sabeena and Madhu were awestruck as Vikram unfolded his entire vision for, The Ramkund Mission over an elaborate lunch in Agra. They knew his potential. 'You are born to do great things,' murmured Sabeena as Vikram took them through his project plan. Both of them were excited to be part of his team.

Vikram insisted that they stay on after lunch and

join his next round of meetings with the architects. Sabeena was floored by the whole idea—an ashram, a training school, research facilities, all amid nature—and asked the designing team many questions and offered suggestions. Vikram was impressed and complimented her for her confident, articulate, leader-like behaviour.

Madhu smiled at Vikram. 'This is not the old Sabeena,' she said, telling him about how Sabeena had been helping everyone in her Basti and in the neighbourhood. She talked about the various camps and seminars Sabeena had been organising of late. Vikram looked at her with reverence and admiration.

Later, Vikram took them for a walk in the hotel garden and told them about his breakup. He looked depressed, tears rising in his eyes.

'Do you still love her?' asked Madhu.

'I would be lying if I said no.'

'You have to get over her.'

'I'm working to forget Eva. It takes time, especially when you love someone so deeply. It's going to take a long time.'

Sabeena did not utter a word. She kept looking at Vikram sympathetically, warmly, as if trying to absorb all his pain. In her silence, the immense love she had for him was plain to see. Sabeena casually stepped aside, plucked a red rose from the garden and quietly tucked it into the top buttonhole of his shirt. She gently told him to go back to his room and relax a bit before his next meeting. Vikram hugged both of them and called the car driver to drive the girls' home.

Sabeena and Madhu returned home with mixed feelings, happy for what they had seen and heard, but sad for what Vikram had endured. Sabeena was worried about his suffering, yet Eva's arrival and departure from Vikram's life did not alter her feelings for him. Her love for Vikram was unilateral, strong and unflinching. In her heart, she was created for Vikram and Vikram only.

Two months later, Vikram held a press conference at the hotel to formally announce the Ramkund Mission project. He declared that the Mission was named after Ramkund, the ancestral town his father had been forced to leave behind in Pakistan. He explained the aims of the Mission, emphasising the inclusive nature of the project.

'The thirty-acre campus will be the first of its kind in our part of the world. The first phase of the campus will already be functional within a year.'

The media coverage created a nationwide buzz. The government expressed support, but a few local politicians, worried that Vikram could emerge as a local power called the project 'a conspiracy against social tranquillity and equilibrium of the region by some hidden foreign forces.'

Vikram responded in the local press, 'Such reactions

from a few local politicians were expected, but I will engage with them and clear their doubts, if any. My effort will be to bring everyone onboard and involve them. I have no interest in politics or power.'

Construction of the mission campus began on a thirty-acre parcel of land between the Tundla railway station and the river Yamuna, about two kilometres from the Quarters. The Sarhadis, Balwant, Madhu and Sabeena would often walk down to watch the progress. Hundreds of new trees were planted and the first operational part of the campus was a grazing ground for animals. Vikram shuttled almost daily between his camp office in Agra and the construction site.

When the campus was completed two years later, it was hailed as an architectural delight. At the heart of the campus was a large, raised *chaupal*, an agora with a green roof sloping over it, supported by crafted pillars, and encircled by hundreds of flowering plants and shrubs, which soon started attracting butterflies. It was designed in a way to offer comfort in both the searing summer heat and the chill of the north Indian winter. Within the first few weeks of its launch, the residents had renamed it: "The Dome".

Ten meeting-cum-lecture rooms, were located seventy meters away from the agora, forming a circle around it, with the identical features—green hip roof, no walls, pillars and the rings of flowering plants. However, these rooms also had basements, all fully equipped with chairs and modern equipment. The soul of the campus were three interlinked artificial lakes, where swans flocked. The campus had office blocks and over one hundred cottages made of basic, earthy material, but well-equipped and comfortable with electricity, a small pantry, hot water, and modern toilets. Each cottage had a small living area, a small study, and a bedroom. A large library and a fitness centre were located within easy access from all the cottages. The community could grow their own food. The agora was used as a prayer space every morning and evening.

By the end of the first year, the Mission had thirty full time employees and over a hundred and twenty in-house researchers-cum-volunteers, called Fellows, Associates and Juniors. They belonged to different parts of the country and beyond. Five Fellows had come from the Middle East and Europe, researching on displaced people. Fifteen Fellows focused on the social issues pertaining to the Scheduled Castes communities.

Recognising her dedication and the name she had earned for herself, Vikram invited Sabeena to join as a full-time manager and a member of The Mission's management team.

'You are the talent we were looking for. This is a recognition of your potential; it is no favour.'

Sabeena locked up her shanty in the Basti and

moved into an allotted cottage on campus. She was given a cottage named *Koel,* which was nine cottages away from Vikram's. Sabeena took to the work and life on the campus like a fish to water, instantly winning the admiration of her fellow workers and volunteers. She worked hard the entire day and every evening, she dropped in at a Research Fellow named Maeve Johanson's cottage to brush up her English. Originally from Ireland, Maeve had come from England and was researching Afghan refugees in India.

Maeve and Sabeena loved the evenings at the campus for the sudden transformation brought in by thoughtfully placed electric lamps, playful animals, and singing birds as they prepared for the night. Chants and prayers at the Dome added to the ambience. Every weekend, earthen lamps replaced the electricity bulbs and songs, dances and short plays happened post dinner. Thursday evenings were dedicated to *'In the Company of Truth'* discussion sessions, with two or three distinguished speakers. Such events were open to all those interested.

The Mission's fellows and volunteers regularly visited Tundla, educating and training, running camps and building communities. They regularly stayed in nearby villages for weeks as part of the strategy to '*Take the Mission to the Villages*'. The Mission's periodicals and publications were widely circulated and became hugely popular.

The Mission's activities and events touched the life of thousands of people in the villages around the Tundla region. And its achievements were often reported in the media all around the country and beyond. Specially designed short-term courses to empower the poor, marginalised women and 'untouchables' were made easily accessible.

Research papers written by the Mission's scholars found appreciation and endorsement from the central and state governments in India, and top universities and think tanks globally, and the Mission attracted hundreds of applications every month from serious scholars. Within a few years of its establishment, the Mission's name and fame travelled across borders and oceans. Vikram had stayed in the background, as he did not want the Mission to be identified with him or any single person.

'I want the Ramkund Mission to live far beyond me. I may have initiated it, but I should not matter,' he often told Sabeena. 'Everything should be about our work, our mission, our goals.'

Vikram's father and Balwant uncle had taken early retirement to join the Mission, with Balwant responsible for security while Sudarshan Sarhadi and his wife were responsible for nutrition and food services. All three reported to Sabeena, who had by then been promoted to a senior executive position.

Sabeena persuaded Balwant and Vikram's parents, who received a monthly pension from the railways, to move onto the campus and allotted them a hut each, which they accepted. Over time, they all grew very fond of Sabeena, now treating her as one of the family.

Vikram worked tirelessly, almost sixteen hours a day, often travelling to New Delhi and overseas to build and promote the Mission. He was both a purist, and an idealist, qualities that sometimes hindered his ability to expand his network. He had, over the past few years, refused offers of financial support from several organisations and companies, whose integrity he found questionable. It took time, but Vikram's clarity and strategy paid off, eventually positioning the Ramkund Mission among the top one hundred reputed charity institutions in the world.

With Vikram's banking expertise, the Mission established a national cooperative bank for the oppressed and marginalised, with Sabeena as its chairperson. Vikram took great pride in Sabeena's emergence as a compelling speaker and brilliant organiser and administrator. If there was one person entirely dedicated to the mission, it was her. At times she appeared even more devoted and passionate than Vikram.

The Ramkund Mission Cooperative Bank was headquartered in Tundla, with an ambitious expansion plan for the next five years. Vikram recruited three experienced bankers from Bombay and New Delhi and set up an operations office in Agra. He also sent Sabeena to attend an advance management training programme for three months at a prestigious business school, in Ahmedabad. She later spent two months at a banking school, in Hyderabad.

The Mission had now become a household name. Full page profiles of the Mission appeared regularly in newspapers and magazines, not only across India, but also in Europe and the United States. Vikram had become a well-known personality in India, though he continued to treat the Mission as a grassroots and regional organisation. In the villages around Tundla, Vikram was revered as a monk. He often undertook journeys to interact with the villagers, understand their problems and help them, however he could. In return, the villagers would often turn up at the campus and leave milk, grains, and pulses to express their gratitude.

Vikram and Sabeena emerged as the public faces of Mission. They often received invitations to speak at conferences and gatherings. One day, they received an invitation from a London-based foundation to attend the 'All Continents Conference on Refugees and Discrimination' in Islamabad, Pakistan. The invite brought great joy to Vikram. He accepted it at once, and asked Sabeena to join him as a panellist. She was thrilled.

However, when he shared the news at home, Sudarshan Sarhadi strongly objected to his son going to Islamabad. 'No way, no way, no way. 'Please no, no … do not go there'. He pleaded. He protested. He made his feelings known as forcefully as he could. Lakshmi also warned her son with great concern, urging him not to go. But Vikram could not be stopped; Opportunities like this did not come often, and the trip to Pakistan would be made at any cost.

20

Vikram and Sabeena had three months to prepare for the journey. They worked very closely on the topics they wanted to discuss at the conference. It was clear that they enjoyed great chemistry and compatibility. Soon enough, everyone on the campus could sense Sabeena's love for Vikram. They walked together frequently in the evenings, often holding hands. Sabeena could also be seen carrying food to Vikram's hut late in the night.

Days before the conference, they left New Delhi for Lahore, enroute to Islamabad. They planned to stay in Lahore before travelling to Islamabad by road. Vikram's parents were deeply worried about this trip, and his mother felt as though she had received a premonition that history would come home to her family when her son crossed the border she had crossed so many years ago.

The flight from New Delhi to Lahore was short, but

it took the pair a long time to clear immigration and customs. The officials had too many questions. Sabeena faced immense scrutiny—a young woman, a Muslim as far as her passport was concerned, travelling alone with a young Hindu man, was enough to sound all kinds of prejudiced alarms.

An immigration official asked Sabeena twice if she had booked a separate room in the hotel. They also asked if she was a practicing Muslim.

'No, I am not,' she said calmly. I am a practicing humanist.'

They walked out with flagging spirits, hoping to rest at the hotel. But the warmth with which a taxi driver, a tall man wearing a loose turban, received them and broke into a monologue about the beauty of Lahore, lifted their spirits. The driver introduced himself as *Germanwala,* an epithet he had received for having spent two years in Munich illegally in an effort to settle there, before he was caught and deported. He chattered endlessly and had seen more Bollywood movies than both Vikram and Sabeena.

He then changed the topic to politics, lambasting the Pakistani army for keeping the country poor and uneducated as part of a conspiracy. 'Keep the people poor and uneducated and then kick them in their backside if they demand anything more. This is what they are doing to Pakistan,' he snapped.

When they got to the hotel, they walked into the lobby, their heads buzzing. Vikram looked around and smiled.

'This is the land of my ancestors. My mother was born here. My grandfather's brother spent his entire life in Lahore. He taught English literature at the Government College. We should visit it tomorrow,' said Vikram to Sabeena over a late dinner.

'Lahore looks a lot like Old Delhi,' Sabeena observed.

Lahore had a charm of its own and was known for its culture, cuisine, clothes, and unique evenings. Lahoris had a popular saying: *Jisne Lahore nai dekhya, o jamyai nai,* meaning, someone who has not seen Lahore has not been truly born.

The couple spent the next day touring the Badshahi Mosque, the majestic Fort and the famous Mall Road and Anarkali Bazaar, a popular shopping street named after Anarkali, Sharif un-Nissa, a courtesan from Lahore in the court of the Mughal Emperor Akbar in the sixteenth century, who, as legend has it, had an illicit relationship with his son, the crown Prince Salim. Vikram bought woollen shawls for his mother, father, and Balwant Uncle at Anarkali Bazar. He also bought a shawl that Sabeena had admired and gifted it to her.

Sabeena was keen to try the delicacies Lahore was known for, so they hopped from place to place enjoying the food. In the evening, they took a leisurely walk in Shalimar Garden.

'It's beautiful!' Sabeena exclaimed unable to contain her excitement, as she gently grabbed Vikram's arm, while they walked on.

Vikram silently enjoyed the loving gesture. He responded by warmly squeezing her hand, surprising Sabeena, who had been lost in the drizzle and mist created by a dancing water jet of a multi-jet fountain. Her heart beating wildly, she leaned against his shoulder. The garden had done what Sabeena had been waiting for all her life; its gentle beauty had awakened Vikram to the tender feelings he nursed for her. He planted a quick kiss on her lips, making her blush deeply. Her soul was alight. Passersby stared at them as they exited the garden, but they didn't care.

Vikram hailed a taxi to get back to the hotel. Sabeena followed Vikram to his room, dragging him to the sofa, slipping into his lap, and entered a world of utter bliss. She returned to her room to change for dinner. She knew he was now in love with her. She was the happiest person in the world.

They left Lahore for Islamabad the next day, after visiting the Government College making an unsuccessful attempt to look for the house where Vikram's mother was born. The neighbours told them that the house had been demolished in the 1960s to make space for a commercial building.

A planned city built in the 1960s, Islamabad had abundant greenery with mountains in the backdrop. Most buildings belonged to the federal government or were foreign embassies. The houses looked large and posh, owned mainly by the country's powerful elite, such as military generals, politicians, and corporate magnates.

The 'All Continents Conference on Refugees and Discrimination' was a massive event. The President of Pakistan delivered the Inaugural Address, followed by that of the country's foreign minister. Both announced strong support for Afghan refugees in Pakistan. They claimed there were over five million refugees in the country since the Soviet Union had occupied Afghanistan in 1979.

Over 700 delegates were present from across the world. Vikram and Sabeena were the only delegates from India. When Vikram stood up to speak as a keynote speaker in a plenary session, he was welcomed with applause, and began by reciting an Urdu couplet from Pakistan's late national poet, Sir Muhammad Iqbal.

He then addressed the audience, '...nothing without roots can survive for long. Everyone has a place they come from. But many, like me, are refugees. My parents are refugees. They were forced to leave their ancestral land because of the Partition. Although they learned to live in their adopted home, Tundla, a small town near Agra, they suffered an immense loss. My father's ancestral home, Ramkund, in North Waziristan, is not that far from here. But he can never return to it. The trauma they went through has been passed on to me. Like my parents, I also yearn for Ramkund, the land of my ancestors. When we force a person to become a refugee, we harm several generations of that family. Every child in a family of refugees is a wounded soul.

'Tundla has given me everything I could have wished for—safety, shelter, education, opportunity. Yet, I feel restless, and lost, because Tundla cannot give me roots in my own land, the soil my ancestors nurtured with their sweat.

'Any person who is denied freedom, dignity and a home is a refugee. A life without justice is not a life at all. Therefore, we must deliberate on these issues as well. We must consider a more comprehensive meaning of the word "refugee". I urge this conference to consider establishing a global foundation for refugees with its headquarters in India, and the Ramkund Mission will be glad to anchor and host such an initiative. Thank you.'

At the end of the speech there was great applause. Sabeena, seated in the front row, smiled with pride. Vikram was surrounded by delegates and journalists as soon as the conference broke up for lunch. He spent hours in interviews. The next morning, Vikram's photo and his statements were splashed across newspapers in Pakistan.

Muhammad Gohar, a prominent figure in North

Waziristan, followed these reports with great interest.

The conference dinner was a feast. Delicious food, expensive wine (only for foreigners), and a musical show were organised for all the delegates.

The next day, Sabeena gave the keynote address at a plenary session. She began by thanking the hosts for the invitation. Unlike Vikram, who was formal and serious, Sabeena's style of presentation was more conversational and informal.

'I have suffered humiliation and oppression all my life. I belong to an untouchable caste, now named Valmiki Dalit, which meant I faced endless discrimination and exploitation. Until a few years ago, I lived in a *basti*—a ghetto of poverty and unhappiness—before I was empowered by education and good luck. Like Vikram Sarhadi, who spoke in the plenary yesterday, I am also a refugee, in the sense that I had to run away to save my life from the neglect and shame of our caste system. Nothing is worse than being at the lowest rung of this caste hierarchy. You battle all your life just to be treated like a human being. I did not travel for days and weeks to save my life. I had to travel only two miles, from my ghetto to the campus of the Mission, but the time it took me to find safe ground was longer than any other refugee might have taken. It may be difficult to escape from the clutches of an oppressive state system, but it is just as difficult to liberate yourself from the hold of an oppressive social system.

Pakistan's 'untouchables' have their own tales to share, and these stories may be as bad if not worse than mine. Things get even worse if you happen to be a woman, and an independent-minded one at that. Denying freedom and dignity to a woman is criminal and against the basic tenets of humanity. Denying a woman her due in society, culture, education, governance, and commerce is a crime against humanity. The world exists thanks to women. The world perpetuates thanks to women. The world lives on thanks to women. So, empower your women, empower the marginalised. See the entire world change into a peaceful and prosperous paradise.'

The loudest applause came from the Pakistani women delegates in the room. A Pakistani minister, seated in the VIP row, went up the dais to congratulate Sabeena for giving an inspiring speech. The media fell in love with Sabeena. Her speech was covered by national and international newspapers. Vikram was thrilled to see the rise of a new, sparkling Sabeena over the course of the conference.

'I am so glad you agreed to come to this conference,' he told her.

'I'm grateful you asked me to come. This has been so liberating.'

'I am happy for you. This is a new Sabeena, taking the world by storm,' Vikram insisted.

'There is no *new* Sabeena,' Sabeena laughed, 'I'm happy and confident because you are with me. I'm happy because you have accepted me.'

After dinner, they went for a drive around Islamabad and returned to the hotel to pack and sleep before their journey to Murree, a mountain resort town thirty kilometres away.

21

Vikram and Sabeena enjoyed the drive from Islamabad to Murree—soaking in the sweet air, bird songs and breathtaking view throughout the journey. They got out twice from the car to view the beautiful mountains and valleys amidst the floating mist and fog.

Vikram had heard so much about Murree from his father. 'When I was a child, Murree was a place in my imagination, a paradise I could never dream of visiting. But now, here I am!'

They checked into the Murree Continental Palace Hotel, just a street away from Mall Road, the heart of the hill town. They went for a walk on Mall Road, enjoying a spell of mild weather. Sabeena had never seen the Himalayas before. She was as exhilarated, as a child. She only knew of such places through Bollywood movies, where actors danced around in such locales. The pair did not talk much, but held each other's hands tight, shared an ice cream bar and planted kisses on each other's shoulders and foreheads.

Known for its neo-gothic architecture, the town of Murree was established by the British in the 1850s as a retreat to escape the heat and dust of Rawalpindi and Lahore during the summer months. Over the decades, many interesting stories had enriched local folklore, including tales of the ghost of a British officer who had died in the 1880s, or a sincere belief that Murree was the place where Mary, the mother of Jesus Christ, was buried.

They returned to the hotel for an early dinner as they intended to sightsee again the next day before heading back to Islamabad for a dinner at the residence of the Indian Ambassador. Vikram then retired to his room, only to respond a few minutes later to Sabeena knocking on his door, smiling.

'I cannot sleep. Let's go to the rooftop and enjoy the sight of the stars over the mountains,' Sabeena smiled. 'They even have a cafe upstairs. We can get some hot chocolate.'

The view from the rooftop felt like looking out into a fairyland. The fog had dispersed, and the crisp air was invigorating. Lights twinkled across the valleys, where people's homes were lit up with lamps. Vikram and Sabeena sat down in a corner, ordering rounds of hot chocolate.

'Do you want to know why I really wanted to come here? My grandfather and grandmother had come here for their honeymoon and stayed for a week. My father was born nine months after. Baba never tires talking of Murree,' said Vikram, sipping hot chocolate. 'Apparently our family even owned a cottage here.'

Sabeena embraced him gently. She then disappeared for some minutes to speak with the housekeeping staff of the hotel, and returned with a grin. 'We are going to sleep here on the rooftop. They close the cafe at midnight, so we will have the entire place to ourselves. It gets colder, but it should be manageable. Housekeeping is arranging a bed and extra blankets. It will be so romantic. We can go back to our rooms if you don't like it or if it gets really cold.'

Soon only Sabeena and Vikram were left on the rooftop, tucked under a blanket in the same bed with only stars in the distant sky for the company. She planted kisses all over his face and his lips. 'You said your grandparents came here for their honeymoon. I can see them in the sky, blessing us,' Sabeena whispered, and gave him a long deep kiss.

Vikram looked at her for long time, as if thanking her profoundly for her love. He pulled her closer and kissed her passionately. 'I love you,' he murmured.

Sabeena was elated. She embraced him and said, 'Vikram, with the stars as our witness, and with your grandparents' blessings from up there, I take you as my husband. *Kabool hai?* Do you accept?'

Vikram was quiet for a moment. He then took Sabeena into his arms and said, '*Haan, sweekar hai,* I accept.'

The couple hugged each other.

They did not sleep all night, and spent it talking, kissing, and making love. They were, for all intents and purpose, husband and wife, and they promised to formalise the marriage once back in Tundla.

'I will never forget Murree in my life. This place has given me everything I ever wanted,' said Sabeena, as they drove back to Islamabad.

The Indian Ambassador and his wife had invited Vikram and Sabeena to dinner after they had seen wide coverage of their speeches in the Pakistani media. The Ambassador welcomed them to his sprawling residence.

'Thanks for accepting our invitation. We know it was at a very short notice.'

They spoke about the conference, and how Vikram and Sabeena were enjoying their time in Pakistan.

'How long are you staying in Pakistan?' the Ambassador's wife asked.

'Four more days. We go to Ramkund in North Waziristan tomorrow morning for two days, back on the third day and return to Delhi.' Vikram nodded.

'Sorry, did you say North Waziristan?' the

Ambassador looked troubled. 'But why?'

'Delegates from an NGO that works among Afghan refugees in the Ramkund area met us at the conference and invited us.'

'Do you know these people from before?'

'No, we met them at the conference for the first time. I wanted to go to Ramkund anyway. Now they have arranged everything,' Vikram said.

'North Waziristan is quite far from here. It might not be safe, are you familiar with the area?'

'Yes, I have been studying the maps of the area since my school days. My family is originally from there.'

The Ambassador looked uncomfortable. He toyed with his food and he then spoke, 'Son, I don't think you should go. Waziristan is a tribal area, and diplomatic protections are difficult to enforce in those regions.'

'I have been dying to go there ever since my father told me about our roots in Ramkund. I want to go and see my ancestral home, *Sarhadi Haveli,* and look at the fields which we owned. It would heal me; it would help me heal the rootlessness I suffer from.'

'You seem to be very emotional about this trip,' cautioned the Ambassador. 'I cannot stop you, but I don't think it's a safe place. However, I must insist that you do not take Sabeena with you. It's definitely not safe for a woman.'

Vikram and Sabeena returned to their hotel, stressed and confused. After thinking hard, Vikram decided to go alone, overruling Sabeena's insistence on accompanying him.

22

Roots NW, the NGO that had introduced itself to Vikram at the conference, had organised two four-wheelers for the eight-hour journey to North Waziristan. Three volunteers accompanied Vikram, among them a young, English-speaking woman. She handed him a bag filled with literature about *Roots* activities and accolades as soon as Vikram settled into the black SUV. The volunteers expressed deep disappointment that Sabeena had not been able to join them.

Vikram had bought extra film rolls to take as many photographs as possible of the *Sarhadi Haveli* and the surrounding fields and areas. Although he was worried because of the Ambassador's warnings, the volunteers put him at ease, and he decided to make the most out of the trip anyway.

North Waziristan was often described as extremely dangerous, especially by Western media. The federal government in Islamabad had little writ over the region, famous for its rugged beauty and entrenched tribalism.

When Vikram asked the volunteer to tell him about North Waziristan, she said, 'All these areas we are motoring through are known for tribalism. We all are tribals here, with our own way of life and traditions. One of our traditions is about revenge. A guest is like a god for us, but an enemy is an enemy—an entity that must be eliminated. Revenge of any kind is serious business here, and is passed on from generation to generation.'

Vikram frowned, wondering why she was talking to him about revenge. An ominous feeling came over him, but he tried not to think too deeply about it.

'Has nothing changed with time?'

'Not in North Waziristan, not in your Ramkund. People still live by old tribal rules, practices and traditions. They have their own unwritten laws.'

'That is quite something. I have been invited to visit the refugees' camps in the area, and obviously that is my priority. But I would also like to visit my ancestral home,' Vikram said.

They stopped at a small roadside restaurant for lunch. Vikram had some corn bread with yoghurt. He noticed he was the only non-local in the restaurant. His overall impression of the journey so far felt eerie and surreal. Vikram also noticed that one of the men escorting him had a pistol under his long shirts. The

Ambassador's warning played in his mind repeatedly.

'Do you need to carry the gun on you?' Vikram asked as they left the place after lunch.

'For safety.' The woman pulled out a German pistol from her brown bag. 'You never know what could happen. Even I have one.'

Soon the sun began its descent behind the dark, rugged mountains. The traffic from the opposite direction often had men in baggy pants and flowing, oversized shirts, wearing flat woollen caps, clutching guns and rifles.

'These men were fighting against the Soviet Union and the communists in Afghanistan. They are warriors,' the volunteer told Vikram. 'Millions of Afghans had to flee their homeland into Pakistan since the Soviets occupied their country.'

Vikram was excited to see an old sign, written in Urdu and English, saying they were now in Ramkund. It was quite dark, with no street lights, and no other lights except for lamps that were lit in some houses in the horizon.

Vikram's momentary excitement after seeing the sign was soon replaced with edginess and anxiety as the SUV came to a sudden stop and the three escorts got down in a hurry without even bidding goodbye. They were replaced by four men armed with automatic machine guns. They did not utter a word and accelerated the vehicle. The other car that had followed them all the way from Islamabad reversed and sped away into the darkness.

Vikram knew he was in trouble.

'Where are you taking me?' he asked.

'Keep quiet,' the one driving ordered. 'Are you the son of Sudarshan Sarhadi?'

Vikram, sensing trouble, tried not to answer. 'But what's the matter?'

'Answer our question first. Are you the son of Sudarshan Sarhadi?'

'Yes, I am. But how do you know my father?'

'You will know soon.'

After driving for thirty minutes, they reached a single-storey house in an isolated area. The house looked like a warehouse. Vikram was shown into a room and ordered to make himself comfortable there for the night. Five gun-toting men patrolled the area to make sure he did not try to escape. He was offered dinner of two slices of Afghan bread and beef curry. He refused to eat and stayed awake the entire night, filled with fear and morbid curiosity. He had been kidnapped, and for what?

'Do they want a ransom? Does this have to do with my nationality? How did they know my Baba's name? Why did they check if I was his son?'

He knew he was in deep trouble. He wished he

had listened to his father's oft repeated advice to never go back to Pakistan. He also regretted ignoring the Ambassador's advice. He spent a restless, cold night, wondering how he would get out of this situation, but also grateful that Sabeena was safely in Islamabad, and not stuck here in Ramkund.

Muhammad Gohar Khan arrived at eight the next morning and invited Vikram to a table arranged in the open for breakfast. He had several bodyguards who patrolled the area in all directions. He introduced himself as a family enemy of the Sarhadis.

'An ancestral enemy?' Vikram wondered aloud. 'We don't even live here anymore. I wanted to come here to see my ancestral home. So, the NGO was your ploy to draw me here.'

'Your family ran the most successful and the richest business in this entire area. You had the biggest house and the highest repute, but what your father did was wrong, and against the established rules of society here,' said Khan quietly.

Muhammad Gohar Khan was a regional lord, an opium peddler and the chief of a dreaded group of militants and terrorists. He was too powerful to care about even the federal government in Islamabad. The government, engaged, behind the scenes in a war with the Soviet Union in Afghanistan, needed him more than he needed them.

'I have to avenge what your father did to the honour of my family. I have to take revenge before I die,' he said in a soft, yet menacing voice. 'We have lived with this shame for too long. For decades.'

'I don't know what you're talking about,' Vikram stammered.

Khan shot him a look of hatred. 'We seven brothers had only one sister. She was the apple of our eyes and the joy of our joint family. Your father seduced her, making her pregnant. We had to kill her to protect our family's honour. She was just sixteen. We took her to a mountain top, shot her dead and buried her there.'

The story stunned Vikram, who sat there like a brick, unable to comprehend what he was hearing.

'We went after your father to kill him the same night we had killed our sister, but your family was rich and very powerful, and managed to protect him from our wrath. We tried again during the Partition riots. We had our best chance to kill him one night; there was blood everywhere. The Hindus were under attack. But your father escaped—he survived. We killed several of his family members. He was lucky that night.'

'Were they in love?' Vikram asked in a daze. 'How can you hold one responsible over the other?'

'It is always the man who is responsible in such situations,' Khan thundered. 'Our sister was innocent. And we still want revenge. A few years ago, I sent a man from Kabul to kill Sudarshan Sarhadi in Tundla, but again he survived.'

'So, it was you who sent that attacker.'

'Yes, he was our man,' Khan replied. 'We punished him for returning without completing the mission. Judging by your reactions, your father did not tell you what he did to us, to our honour. Otherwise, you would not have dared to come here. Your father may have forgotten, but it is still fresh in our minds. Family honour is a serious business. Revenge is a serious matter. Our girls do not love or marry outside our tribe. Sarhadi destroyed our reputation. He will be punished.' Khan flicked his fingers in dismissal.

The guards took Vikram back to his room and locked the room from outside. He asked for a piece of paper to write a note for Sabeena, but the guards ignored him. The windows in the room were firmly closed from the outside. He was left alone, with no food, no water, and no toilet.

At midnight, two men in black clothes entered his room, instructing him to board a waiting car outside. There were more men in the vehicle, all heavily armed. They drove for about fifteen minutes, climbing up a mountain. Then they stopped, got out, and ordered Vikram to follow them. It was dead quiet all around. Vikram tripped and fell on the way, and the men in black shouted at him and dragged him the rest of the way.

Muhammad Gohar Khan was already waiting at the top of the mountain. He was also dressed in all black, holding an American pistol in his right hand. He pointed to the spot where Vikram was made to stand and said, 'We killed our sixteen-year-old sister right here. I have brought you here to kill you exactly on the same spot.'

Shivering, Vikram whispered a soft prayer, and thought about Sabeena. He closed his eyes.

Khan murmured something, looked upward, and then pulled the trigger, pumping five bullets into Vikram's heart and head, killing him on the spot.

Vikram's bullet-riddled body was dragged down the mountain, bundled into the boot of the car, and then left in front of *Sarhadi Haveli*, which still bore the same name, but was now owned by a bank.

Muhammad Gohar Khan saw to it that all of Ramkund and North Waziristan knew who the dead person was and why he was punished. Many queued up to congratulate Khan at his fortress-like home for upholding tradition. The local police, more loyal to Khan than the administration, handled the entire matter very casually, misinforming their bosses and the federal government in Islamabad. They declared the death 'a killing by some foreign enemy' without any investigation or probe.

The Indian Ambassador and his wife reached

Islamabad Hotel as soon as they got the news, to meet Sabeena. She looked dazed, almost half-dead. She did not utter a word. The Ambassador left for the Pakistani Foreign Office leaving his wife behind to look after her, issuing instructions not to let the media in. The Ambassador then addressed a press conference, demanding permission for Indian investigative agencies to probe the murder. Pakistan rejected the demand, claiming that Pakistan's agencies would investigate the matter and share the report with India.

The murder shocked India. It shocked millions in Pakistan, too.

Muhammad Gohar Khan's name was not mentioned in the First Information Report by the police despite everybody, including the Pakistani media, clearly identifying him as the murderer.

'Khan is too important an asset for Pakistan's rulers to be given up for the murder of an ordinary Indian man,' editorialised a reputed Urdu newspaper.

Another newspaper criticised the lack of governance in Waziristan. 'There is no government, no rule of law, no police, no justice.'

Two days later, Sabeena, clad in a white cotton sari and looking ten years older, left Islamabad for Delhi with Vikram's casket in the airplane's baggage hold. Pakistan had offered an air force plane to carry the mortal remains, but the Indian Ambassador had turned down the offer.

Thousands turned up at Delhi airport to receive the mortal remains, shouting '*Shahid* Vikram *amar rahe.* Long live the martyr, Vikram.'

23

It was as if the Sarhadi family had been hit by lightning. Lakshmi had to be admitted to the ICU. Neha was also in the same hospital, unconscious. Sudarshan appeared as if he had lost all balance—physical, emotional, mental. Balwant and Madhu were running around trying to hold things together, but were themselves shattered.

Sudarshan blamed himself for everything, screaming, 'I should have been killed!' The Sarhadi family, which counted itself among the most privileged and prosperous until a few days ago, was now in pieces.

'They killed my innocent son! They should have killed me! Why Vikram?'

Balwant tried to calm Sudarshan down, attempting to guide his thoughts towards spirituality, but Sudarshan was too shocked and shaken to have any space for such discussions. His world had collapsed again. Eventually, he stood up and ran across the Company Garden to the railway station and boarded a train for Varanasi without any belongings, wanting to repent and die.

The Mission's campus bore the look of a graveyard—the birds vowed silence, cows stopped mooing, trees stood horrified and the night jasmines stood lifeless, abandoning all their beauty and fragrance. Hundreds of people arrived at the campus, crying, inconsolable.

The volunteers went around the campus lighting lamps everywhere. Special prayers were held in temples, mosques and churches throughout the region. Thousands took to the streets, with candles in their hands and prayers on their lips, demanding justice for the young man who had lived for the poor, vulnerable and the discriminated.

A group of young women organised non-stop prayers at the Dome. All campus residents wore white, the colour of mourning and peace. A special train with a WP steam locomotive and a white carriage left New Delhi station for Tundla in the morning carrying Vikram's remains in a cooled glass case, layered with night jasmine flowers inside and out. Sabeena, clad in all-white, sat next to it, surrounded by about thirty Mission volunteers and well-wishers. Several high-level representatives of the Indian government were also there.

Sabeena organised everything in line with Vikram's passions. She arranged for the train to stop at all major junctions along the way, including Khurja and Aligarh. A group of Sufis sang melodies as the train stopped at the Khurja station. Thousands turned up to bid farewell, many holding small baskets of night jasmine flowers. Sabeena cried uncontrollably every time she saw people offering the flowers to the coffin. Thousands of students from the Aligarh Muslim University turned up at the station to pay their last respects to Vikram.

Sabeena had not moved away from Vikram's coffin. The world she built had come crashing down. She would have to rebuild her world again, and this time without Vikram holding her hand. She looked distraught, but stayed in command of everything around her, as Vikram would have wanted.

Seeing how she conducted herself despite her grief, many people had remarked, 'I can see a great leader in her.'

The Indian and Pakistani media broke the news that the two had been set to marry as soon as they returned from Islamabad.

The train finally reached Tundla Junction—the railway station Vikram loved. Thousands of men and women and children awaited Vikram weeping openly. The police were deployed in large numbers, but they too joined the mourners.

Vikram's body was transported to the Mission in a specially designed casket. The cart moved slowly towards the campus, followed by the mourners. It took the procession two hours to cover the short distance between the railway station and the campus as people kept turning up at every step, insisting on offering prayers and flowers.

The entire country joined Sabeena in her tragedy.

Vikram's body was to be buried in an area between the Dome and the campus's main entrance gate, beside his favourite night jasmine garden. The ground was dug and filled up with two feet of fresh night jasmine flowers, sprinkled with holy water from the Ganges. The Constitution of the Mission was placed under Vikram's head.

Vikram's mother was still in the intensive care unit of the Agra hospital, but Neha, inconsolable, was brought in by Madhu. Sabeena, with swollen eyes and a drawn face, sat between Madhu and Neha. She took out from her bag a long hand written letter addressed to Vikram and carefully placed it on the right side of his chest.

A sea of humanity watched as Vikram was laid to rest for eternity.

A few weeks later, the Governing Committee of the Mission decided to appoint Sabeena as the Chairperson of the Mission and all other associated bodies, including the bank. Reluctantly accepting the offer, Sabeena said that her life henceforth would be completely dedicated to all that Vikram had stood for.

Sabeena threw herself into the Mission's work. To her shock and joy, she discovered that she was pregnant. She immediately visited Vikram's mother, who was now living on the campus as a volunteer, and shared the news. Neha and Madhu were also informed. They hugged each other in joy. Sabeena had already shared the story of her 'marriage under the stars' with them. Sabeena, Neha, Madhu and Lakshmi went to the Hanuman temple to thank Him for the development.

Sabeena wanted to formally marry Vikram at his grave in a ceremony conducted by a Hindu priest. The priests attending the Dome, refused, arguing that the holy texts did not allow marriage to a dead person.

'I do not regard Vikram dead. He is and will always be alive for me,' pleaded Sabeena.

'I respect your love for him, but this cannot be done.'

Nine other priests refused to conduct such a marriage, leaving Sabeena frustrated and heartbroken.

'I do not want our child to be called illegitimate. I want this marriage as soon as possible and in the right Hindu way and tradition,' she shared with Madhu, asking her to find a priest.

Madhu, who had married a Brahmin, said that she would get her husband to do the needful.

The next week, Sabeena was formally married to Vikram at his grave amidst Vedic chants and rituals. Lakshmi, Neha, Madhu and all the campus residents attended the ceremony, which was followed by a simple but sumptuous dinner, with all of Vikram's favourite dishes.

Under the same stars that had been witness to their union, Sabeena formally changed her name to Sabeena Vikram Sarhadi.

Acknowledgment

I owe thanks to Samyuktha Iyer, Cora Bhatia, Reena Singh and Annika Taneja for their support and scrupulous reading and editing of the manuscript. I owe special thanks to Kabir Taneja, who read the first raw draft of the first chapter and encouraged me to press ahead, and Saumya at the Vitasta Publishing for her patience and endless assistance.

